"So how do we get out

Chase gave a heavy sigh.

Lexi chose her words carefully. "The next year, finances will be tight. No matter how badly you want to, or how much it could help others, you can't give out free rooms to the nonprofit. If we leave the lodge open, we need every inch of space filled with paying customers."

He growled. "That's not a solution, Lexi. That's staying stuck."

She didn't know if she would be able to say the words she had planned to say.

"Well..." The word croaked out, and she paused to swallow. "There is one thing. But it might be a sacrifice."

He opened his arms wide. "Anything. I'll do anything to keep the ranch and resort in motion to get the nonprofit fully functional."

Sweat broke out across her brow. Her mouth went dry. "This might—" her heart pounded "—sound unexpected. A little, um, illogical. All things considered."

"Lexi," he said with impatience.

She bit her lip, released it, looked straight into his questioning hazel eyes and said, "You could marry me."

Award-winning author **Deborah Clack** is a native Texan who believes in the power of fiction, the lost art of lip-synching and that chocolate should be eaten without nuts. A high school AP history teacher for ten years, Deborah earned a master's degree in education and was awarded Teacher of the Year for Arts in Education. Now she creates stories of her own filled with endearing characters and hard-fought romances. She would love to connect with you at deborahclack.com.

Books by Deborah Clack

Love Inspired

The Cowboy's Marriage Bargain

Visit the Author Profile page at LoveInspired.com for more titles.

The Cowboy's Marriage Bargain

DEBORAH CLACK

LOVE INSPIRED
INSPIRATIONAL ROMANCE

LOVE INSPIRED
INSPIRATIONAL ROMANCE

Recycling programs
for this product may
not exist in your area.

ISBN-13: 978-1-335-59749-6

The Cowboy's Marriage Bargain

Copyright © 2024 by Deborah Clack

For questions and comments about the quality of this book, please contact us
at CustomerService@Harlequin.com.

® is a trademark of Harlequin Enterprises ULC.

Love Inspired
22 Adelaide St. West, 41st Floor
Toronto, Ontario M5H 4E3, Canada
www.LoveInspired.com

Printed in Lithuania

MIX
Paper | Supporting
responsible forestry
FSC® C021394

For the mountains shall depart, and the hills be removed; but my kindness shall not depart from thee.
—*Isaiah* 54:10

For anyone with the last name Clack, Long, Hardt, Jordan, Longoria, Alley and Patton who has walked with me on the road to publication. We did it! I'm so grateful to call you my family.

Acknowledgments

Thank you to Sami Abrams, Lynn Blackburn, Laura Chen, Kelly Jo Fernandez, David Friedli, Lynne Gentry, Debb Hackett, Sarah Hepola, Kerry Johnson, Bethany Kaczmarek, Sherrinda Ketchersid, Kay Learned, Allyson West Lewis, Shelli Littleton, Julie Marx, Rebekah Millet, DiAnn Mills, Ann Neumann, Tina Radcliffe, Kelly Scott, Stacy Simmons, Becky Wade, Becca Whitham, and Ann Vande Zande. Each of you played monumental roles in gently pushing (some of you shoving) me out of the nest.

Thank you to my father and legal consultant, Bruce Long, and my mother-in-law and medical consultant, Debby Clack. All mistakes in the manuscript are mine, but you still have to keep me around.

Melissa Endlich, working with you is a gift to me.

Tamela Hancock Murray, thank you for your steadfast encouragement.

Lance, I love you. T and M, you are the best cheerleaders on the planet.

Thank you, Lord. To Your glory. Every word, always, to Your glory.

Chapter One

Chase Cross knew better than to tell a woman she looked like a wet dog. Especially the annoyingly precise and beautiful accountant for Four Cross Ranch, the sprawling acreage he owned with his siblings outside of Elk Run, Wyoming.

He leaned his shoulder on the doorjamb to the lodge as Lexi Gardner hurried through the spring rain. She pounded up the stairs to the spacious wraparound covered porch, hugging a three-ring binder to her chest.

The black binder never meant good news. Instead, Chase knew as certainly as he knew the cows would calve soon that she was going to start today's meeting with, "We have a problem."

She skidded to a stop in front of him, cold air puffing out of her mouth. Her enticing floral perfume wafted into his space. "Are you going to stand in my way, or may I please come inside before I catch pneumonia?"

Her attitude set his teeth on edge, but not as much as her words.

She'd stood in his way for the last two years, shutting down his dreams for the family property. From the first time they clashed over budget issues, he had wondered if instead of trying to create a nonprofit on the ranch, he should just reenlist in the army. The United States military had less red tape than the infuriating Miss Lexi Gardner.

"Good morning to you, too," he murmured as he tipped his cowboy hat and shifted for her to enter.

It was unfortunate that his golden retriever liked her. Duke welcomed her with a wagging tail and wide smile, then escorted her inside.

Walking down the hall, pride washed over Chase as he took in what his family had built. Rustic rugs covered the wide-planked wood floors. Paintings of the Old West adorned the walls. Cozy bedrooms awaited guests.

Now if they could get Four Cross Hope, the nonprofit for veterans, up and running, he could feel like he was making a difference in the world again.

Though Wyoming was the least populated state in America, it ranked the ninth largest in square miles. The vast land was the perfect place for veterans to find peace, quiet and open space. Skirting the edge of a national forest with Elk Mountain in the backdrop, the property included acres of rolling prairie that beckoned to those in need of healing.

Today was the day Lexi would tell him that he and his siblings could finally move forward with the nonprofit's long-term plan. The anticipation tasted sweet.

Though Lexi walked next to him, she stared at the ground, her face drawn as if she carried a heavy burden.

His chest tightened.

It always bothered him when he cared about her well-being. He couldn't seem to help himself. Being concerned for her was as automatic to him as being annoyed with her.

"Everything okay?" he asked.

Her head shot up, locks of damp sandy blond hair sticking to her round cheeks. Confusion filled her deep brown eyes, almost as if she'd forgotten he was there. She nodded once. "Yes. Fine."

He stopped at the entrance to the back half of the lodge, a

vast space that included a great room with oversized leather chairs and a chambray-covered couch facing a stone fireplace. Nearby sat a long, sturdy dining table next to an open kitchen where guests could mix and mingle while meals were prepared. He loved this room and couldn't wait for it to be filled with people. But first he had to get through this meeting.

"That's about the fifteenth 'fine' I've heard from you this month," he said.

"Then I must be fine." She wiped the wet strands of hair off her cheeks and stepped past him.

This was one of the reasons he wouldn't marry again. Ask a woman a question, and you never got a straight answer. Clearly, she wasn't fine. And hadn't been fine in several months. But every time he tried to ask her about it, she shut him down.

As he crossed the room, his eyes skittered across the black-and-white photographs framed on the wall. His gaze stopped on the same picture it always did.

A woman on skis, face determined, flying midair over a mogul.

Laura. His wife. His gorgeous, unassuming, adventurous and deceased wife.

No. He would never marry again. He wouldn't survive if he lost someone else.

Chase wrapped a hand around the back of his neck, hung his head and took a deep breath to shake off the heavy feeling. Still imagining his wife's smile, he walked to the sideboard and poured himself a cup of coffee into a black mug with the Four Cross Ranch logo.

A familiar slap on his back jerked him out of the moment, causing the hot drink to slosh onto his shirt.

He righted himself, then glared at his twin, the man who

was his opposite in every way except the image that stared back at him in the mirror. "Watch it, Hunter."

Never one to use a lot of words, Hunter lifted his chin in greeting.

Chase grabbed a napkin and wiped the coffee off his plaid flannel shirt. It was what his wife used to refer to as his rancher uniform. Jeans, thermal undershirt, flannel long-sleeved shirt and boots. Always boots. Just like the army, only now with a cowboy flair.

Lexi placed stapled packets of papers in front of five of the dark leather chairs that stood sentry around the massive oak table. Bold capital letters at the top of the cover page announced the current financial report.

Running cattle on the ranch side of the property was good, honest work, it just didn't fulfill his desire to help others since he left the military. But his retirement checks couldn't pay for his dreams on their own. He needed the green light from Lexi to use ranch funds toward the nonprofit.

Lexi straightened papers at exact right angles to each corresponding chair, then looked up. "Has anyone heard from Ryder?"

Hunter shook his head once. No surprise that Hunter hadn't talked to their little brother.

"My guess is he's still on the bull riding circuit, but will be home when the calves come," said Chase.

She scrunched her nose, something he only admitted to himself he thought was cute. "Maybe I need to schedule a meeting when he's in town to give him an update."

"He handed his proxy to me when he left." Along with a whole host of problems. Chase poured a cup of coffee for Lexi, this mug a pale pink with the ranch logo. "He doesn't get to have feelings about how it's going here if he doesn't care enough to stay."

"Still, he's your brother," she said in a quiet voice.

Steam from the coffee rose out of the cup and disappeared into the air. Just like Ryder seemed to do after each short visit. Chase grabbed three sugar packets. "He is our little brother." He ripped the packages open and poured the sugar, watching the granules dissolve like late winter snow. "I love him. But he's still not here."

She cleared her throat. "Will Cora be attending?"

The thought of his brave little sister made him shake his head. They all had a hand in raising Cora after their parents died. Raised by wolves, she claimed. Then a wolf almost claimed her. "I don't think she's going to set foot on the ranch unless someone is birthing a baby."

"Well, she is the most highly sought-after midwife in town," Lexi said.

Smiling proudly at the thought, he poured creamer into the cup. "She's fearless."

Chase pulled a peppermint out of his pocket, unwrapped it and dropped it into the coffee. He walked the pink mug across the room and handed it to Lexi.

A flash of surprise crossed her face.

Why she was surprised, he'd never know. He always made her a coffee the way she liked it if he was around. Even started carrying peppermints in his pockets. This time, however, her face seemed conflicted.

"Thank you," she said quietly.

He narrowed his eyes at her, and her gaze darted away. The last time he'd handed her a cup, she asked him if he'd laced it with poison. Today she merely thanked him? Something was definitely wrong.

"Not sharing your coffee with me?" his twin asked.

"We shared a womb. Does that mean I'm required to bring you coffee the rest of our lives?"

A smile tipped at the corner of his mouth. "As I recall, I kicked you out of that womb," Hunter muttered as he fixed his own cup of joe.

"Didn't you already have a cup down at the chow hall?" The ranch employed a cook who fed the ranch hands three squares a day in a building on-site. She'd declared Mondays Breakfast Burrito Day, and he knew his brother wouldn't miss it.

"I'm not the one who can't hold my coffee," Hunter murmured.

Chase would have defended himself, but then he looked at Lexi. She'd put her coffee down and was wringing her hands, a show of nerves from the normally confident woman. He might not agree with many of the things she said, and she might raise the hackles on his neck during most of their interactions, but he didn't like to see her in distress. He cared for her.

Kind of. Mostly. In an employer-and-employee way. Or possibly as a friend, on the rare occasion they got along.

She sat down, opened her copy of the financial report and tucked the first page behind the staple. But seconds later, she returned the cover sheet to the top.

The more stressed-out she seemed, the more something in his gut burned.

He caught Hunter's attention and sent a silent message to his twin. Hunter studied Lexi, then flicked his eyes back to him. He agreed. Something was off.

Both men dropped into their chairs and faced Lexi. She glanced at Hunter, then at him, her eyes holding a touch of fear.

Chase leaned forward. "You going to tell us what's going on, Lexi, or do we need to guess?"

Lexi Gardner pushed a piece of damp hair behind her ear, wishing she had something she could use to tie her hair back. She probably looked like a wet dog after running through the rain. Fortunately, her trusty old Civic had gotten her safely from her small rental house off Main Street all the way out to the country. Soon, she'd have to bargain with the town mechanic for a set of new brakes. A task for another day.

She clasped her hands around her warm mug and inhaled the peppermint aroma, hoping it would calm her nerves. Maybe if she spilled her coffee on the financial report, it would erase the dismal results.

Finally, she said, "We have a problem."

Hunter grunted.

Chase glared.

The twins resembled two cars of the same model, only wired differently under the hood. Both ruggedly handsome, they had brute mountain man appeal, six foot two inches of height and a daring look behind their hazel eyes, the weight of the family ranch on their shoulders. But Hunter believed everything would work out fine, whereas Chase wanted all the details nailed down and pursued accordingly.

Still, the two were close. And as hard as it was to wrangle the four Cross siblings together to talk about the financials of the ranch, she found herself envious of their family. In spite of their parents' deaths, they still had each other.

All Lexi had was two ex-fiancés, an estranged mother and a high stakes last will and testament left by her grandmother.

At least Duke liked her, which probably infuriated Chase. She ran a hand over the dog's golden coat for courage.

Refocusing on the twins, she went on. "When you all decided to use the lodge to start a nonprofit, you laid out specific financial goals."

"Yes." Chase nodded, his tone already impatient. "We didn't want to take on a huge loan. Profits from the newly added ranch revenue streams would fund the adjustments we needed to convert the lodge for guests, as well as fund the following year's goals. We've been over this and we're on target for the year. Which is why we made modifications to the lodge and have our first veteran and his wife arriving next week."

Internally, she cringed. With dozens of freelance accounting jobs in three of the surrounding counties, giving tough news to a client wasn't new to her. But she had a soft spot for Four Cross Ranch, even if Chase Cross came with the territory.

"We *were* on target. The money the ranch invested in the development of the lodge worked in the beginning."

"But…" His word weighed heavy.

She looked him in the eye. No matter how much he grated on her last nerve, she owed it to him to give the information straight. That was her job. "We didn't hit our goals the last quarter. Any of them."

Chase rested his elbows on his knees and ran his hands through his short brown hair but said nothing.

"We had no way of predicting the early freeze last fall." The freeze killed the natural vegetation, which meant they used their hay inventory earlier than planned. When the price of feed skyrocketed, every rancher in the area was busting their budget to get their cattle fed.

"I'm so tired of the success or failure of our ranch being dependent on the weather," Chase muttered.

She softened her tone. "The biggest period of risk, we all agreed, was this first year leading to the lodge opening. There was no way to predict the rise of construction costs, old pipes rotting and that we'd lose a crop of hay. The loss of revenue from the significant head of sick cattle was the final straw."

"It's like the ten plagues of Egypt," Chase said. "Only instead of frogs and locusts, it's the ten plagues, rancher's edition."

She hated it when he did that.

He tended to joke through tough situations. It put everyone around him at ease. But watching him closely over the last two years, pain sometimes laced those jokes, and she could see it etched now in the creases that lined his eyes.

The temptation to say something comforting rose in her throat but stopped abruptly. The truth clogged any words that wanted to come out.

After laying out the financials for the men, she sat back. "I'm sorry. But we have to cancel the nonprofit's next growth phase. Instead of housing veterans and building more cabins, we need to concentrate on paying the bills for the ranch. We are one mistake or bad weather incident away from the entire operation going under. We have to stabilize things first if we're going to move forward in any way."

Hunter nodded, shifting his gaze out the window.

Chase speared her with a death glare. "You want us to completely let go of the nonprofit?"

"We can't do it, Chase. I know you're slated for the builder to start early next year to expand Four Cross Hope, but Four Cross Ranch can't afford it. You could barely pay the ranch hands as it was. And my professional suggestion is to use the converted lodge for paying guests instead. For profit." Cold seeped into her bones despite her jeans, thermal shirt and secondhand puffer vest. Maybe buying used clothes didn't always translate to warmth. Handing out bad news to clients didn't, either.

Chase made a fist, set it on the table and leaned toward her. "That's unacceptable, Lexi. It's not just about the couple arriving next week. I already have soldiers planning to come here to recover when they return from deployment. Additional military families, desperate for support, are waiting in the wings."

Heat hit her face. She hated being the numbers person when he talked about his passion to help veterans. It was one thing to offer a local artist free accounting services in exchange for her work on the beautiful antler chandelier in the room. This was something completely different. "We don't have the financial capacity to take it on."

"What about the tax benefits that come with having the nonprofit on the property? All of that was laid out in the plan." A hint of uncertainty underlined his tone. "Or the other arms of the ranch that were supposed to support the cause."

"Yes." She took a sip from her mug, but the conversation embittered the taste of the coffee. "In theory, the farming and ranching was going to support the dining options. Activities like horseback riding and the Little Wranglers program would fund the staffing for guided tours and massage appointments. The list of how we use our existing resources is quite impressive. And yes—in theory, the nonprofit status would have benefited us financially."

His eyes seared into hers, and she almost couldn't continue.

"But if we can't make a significant profit from the ranch," she whispered, "we can't fund the nonprofit side."

"Well… I've already started," Hunter declared.

Dread crawled up her spine. Slowly, she turned to him. In a controlled voice, she asked, "What does that mean?"

Lexi only advised the family on how best to use their money. She had no control over what the members spent daily.

"I bought two pups," he said unrepentantly.

Chase had the audacity to shake his head and chuckle.

"How much did you—"

Hunter held up a hand, the calluses of hard work in her view. "I purchased them with my own dime. I'm going to train them as therapy dogs whether we use them for the veterans and the nonprofit business or not." He pushed to stand. "And all due respect, I need to get back to work now."

"I'm sorry," she said with regret.

"No reason to be. You're just doing your job." He nodded, gave a chin lift to his twin and left the room.

Rain pelted against the windows, and for a few seconds, Chase stared at her in silence.

He leaned back in his chair and cocked his head. "What aren't you saying?"

Sitting ramrod straight, she shifted her focus to the stapled sheets. "I think it would be best if we went over the information in the report."

"I don't want to look at the report. I want you to say the words."

A defensive streak ran up her spine. "I don't know why I prepare for meetings with you guys. Half of you don't show, and the other half, I suspect, use my reports as animal feed."

"If we did, it would certainly save us some money."

She must have looked shocked because Chase's expression filled with remorse, and he shook his head.

"I'm sorry, Lexi. That was uncalled for." He scrubbed a hand down his face and stood. "I'm just frustrated."

His vulnerability stopped her hurt feelings in their tracks. Instead, all she could feel was sympathy.

She was squelching his dream.

Even if they didn't see eye to eye on most things, his passion for military veterans was noble. Honorable.

Which is why for months, she'd been considering the unfathomable.

After pacing the room twice, he approached her and crossed his arms over his chest. "Give me some good news. How do we get back on track?"

She wished he understood how desperately she wanted to fix this problem and how far she was willing to go to help him. But she worried that he might think she was ridiculous if she made the suggestion that'd been rattling around in her head the last few months. Even if the solution she offered would solve significant problems for both of them, he might throw her out on her head anyway.

She tapped two fingers rapidly on the table. "There's one bank who might consider giving us a loan."

He covered her hand with his, stopping the noise and movement, then pulled back. "You know we don't want to go in that direction. Plus, my guess is you're going to tell me we probably won't qualify."

She offered him a wry smile. "You always were the smart one."

"I'm not the smart one. Cora's the smart one," he said about the sister he adored. "I'm the nice one."

"Cora's the astute one." She pointed to him. "You're the mean one."

"Only to you." She scoffed at him, but he continued. "To others, I'm not mean. I'm clever."

"Oh, please. Now you're the delusional one. Ryder is clever," she said. "You're the responsible sibling."

"I am." He splayed his hands on his lean hips and blew out a heavy sigh. "I'm the responsible sibling. So how do we get out of this?"

Her stomach clenched in a way she knew she couldn't ignore. She chose her words carefully. "For the next year, finances will be tight. No matter how badly you want to, or how much it could help others, you can't give out free rooms to the nonprofit. If we leave the lodge open, we have to let go of the nonprofit and instead fill every inch with paying customers."

He growled. "That's not a solution, Lexi. That's leaving war-torn veterans and their families in the lurch."

Acid rose from her stomach up her throat. She didn't know if she would be able to say the words.

"Well…" The word croaked out, and she paused to swallow. "There is one thing."

He opened his arms wide. "Anything. I'll do anything to get the nonprofit fully functional."

Sweat broke out across her forehead. "This might—" her heart pounded "—sound unexpected. A little…um, illogical. All things considered."

"What is it, Lexi?" he asked with impatience.

She looked straight into his hazel eyes and said, "You could marry me."

Chapter Two

Every nerve ending in Chase's body came to attention. He hadn't felt this way since being close range to enemy fire on the battlefield. Dropping his voice low, he enunciated each word. "What did you just say?"

Lexi's eyes widened, and her face paled.

He wasn't sure he'd ever seen the color go out of her rosy cheeks, but he couldn't concern himself with that right now.

"I, um—" She cleared her throat. "I know it sounds weird—"

"Repeat the words, please, Lexi. I need to make sure I heard you correctly."

She shook her head. "Of course you would make me repeat it. Nothing's ever easy with you."

Ignoring her jab, he crossed his arms over his chest and waited.

She huffed out a breath and stared him directly in the eyes. "I said that you could marry me."

The air in the room was completely still. The rain even seemed to silence.

Closing her eyes, she continued quickly. "As a solution to the financial issues with Four Cross Ranch and to get Four Cross Hope funded. You could marry me."

He felt as if she'd lobbed a grenade and it was coming at him in slow motion.

"Explain," he grunted.

Her eyes shot open, this time with a familiar fire behind them. "My grandmother left me a trust. A significant amount of money. I'll be granted access to the entire fund on my thirty-fifth birthday with one condition."

Everything in him blanched. "You're a trust fund baby?"

"What?" She reared back, her tone shocked. "No."

He hated people who had things handed to them easy. There was something disingenuous about it. "Sounds like you're about to become an heiress on your thirty-fifth birthday."

She rested her elbows on the table and leaned her face on her hands. "I'm *not* an heiress. And I may not get the money, according to my grandmother's wishes."

The picture of a frail, elderly woman in hospice popped up in his memory. Deep-veined hands and a raspy breath. But her eyes had held the same fire as her granddaughter's. "Is this the grandmother I met? Louella Chadwick?"

"Yes."

The woman was as eccentric as she was kind and wise. Chase thought she said outrageous things just to make him laugh. He'd enjoyed his time with her.

The side of his mouth hitched up. "She was a trip."

"I believe you told me you knew I was related to her because she said nonsensical things like me."

Amused, he grinned. "Sounds like something I would say."

"She liked you," she said.

He shook his head. "That doesn't make sense. You and I fought the entire visit over a stupid tray of hospital food. I still can't believe you let her eat that stuff."

"It's what she ordered. I was just glad she had an appetite."

The reminder of the elderly woman's last days hung heavy between them. So did whatever was pushing Lexi to propose to him. He wanted to see the spark back in her eyes. Experience the bolt of lightning she could be. "What made your grandmother change her mind about me?"

Lexi's eyes flashed.

Good. He wanted to see more of that.

"I told her you were more than just your pretty face," she said dryly.

He cocked his head, ready to give her a hard time right back. "You think my face is pretty?"

"No. I lied so she would feel better."

"A worthy cause."

Lexi sighed. "She said she liked how you challenged me."

If her grandmother only knew how much the reverse was true. He gentled his voice. "I'm sorry you lost her."

"I had only just found her again." Her eyes glistened. "I didn't even get a chance to ask her what I really wanted to know."

Chase didn't know the whole story.

When Lexi showed up in town two years ago, she stuck like glue to her grandmother for the final six weeks of her life. By the time he'd met Ms. Chadwick, she was only days from her last breath. And with Lexi new in town, she was in need of a friend. Elk Run might be Chase's hometown, but he had recently moved back and felt a little unsure himself. He might have needed a friend as well.

But just days after her grandmother's funeral, Lexi put up an impenetrable wall. Maybe it was the grief that overtook her. He understood all too well the things grief could destroy.

All he knew now was that they'd been fighting ever since.

Lexi stood and walked to the windows. She rubbed her arms as if trying to warm herself.

He needed to steer them back to their original conversation. "You mentioned there was a condition to getting access to the trust."

Her eyes were aimed at the window but appeared unfocused. She mumbled something he couldn't understand.

He stepped closer to her. "What did you say?"

She looked at him. "I have to be married on my thirty-fifth birthday in order to access the funds."

Realization hit him square in the chest. "And you think we should get married?"

"I don't—" She rubbed her forehead. "I *don't* think we should get married. No one who knows us thinks we should get married."

That sounded about right. Everyone who knew them had seen them spar at one point or another. Sometimes for fun. Sometimes for not-so-fun. "Then why did you ask?"

"I didn't ask," she said, her voice raised and her face red. "I added up the numbers. I'm an accountant. It's what I do."

"What does that mean exactly?"

"This entire situation is an equation." She paced like a caged animal alongside the table. "There are only a few ways to solve it. I offered you one possible solution to your problem. Marry me, and the money from the trust can help every aspect of Four Cross Ranch."

"Why in the world would you offer up this option? You must have other prospects." People who didn't cringe when they saw her walking toward them. Men who actually wanted to spend the rest of their lives with her.

She stood straighter and lifted her chin. "I'd rather not discuss that right now, if that's all right with you."

"No." He scoffed and ran a hand through his hair. An

anger he didn't quite understand began to simmer just under the surface. "It's not all right with me. I don't want to get married again, Lexi. I've said that to you before. Why in the world would you pick me?"

Without moving a muscle in her body, she stared at him, but said nothing.

He swung his arms out in the direction his brother had gone earlier. "Hunter. You could have asked Hunter. Since he only mutters a few words at a time, you'd have less chance of disagreeing with everything that comes out of his mouth."

"Hunter has a girl in town who's sweet on him. They've had dinner a few times over the years. I'm not going to step on someone else's territory."

Confusion almost knocked him sideways. "Hunter has a girlfriend?"

"If you looked up from your work every now and then, you might have noticed he isn't always at dinner."

Chase stared through the window across the field as if he could see Hunter's social life. "Hunter's seeing someone?"

She sighed and walked to the table. "I don't think it's serious, but I get the impression she would like it to be more."

"Who is it?"

"If you think I'm going to subject an innocent woman to a Chase Cross interrogation, you've got another think coming." She pointed her index finger to the ground. "And I don't care if you are twins. Hunter gets to have a separate life from you if he wants to."

Her words struck a chord. "I'm fairly certain I know that better than anyone else, seeing as how he left the military long before I did." They'd been twenty-six years old at the time, both living their dream of serving their country. After their parents had died in a car wreck, Hunter's insistence that he return home to take care of their younger siblings, then teenagers, still plagued Chase with guilt.

"What about Ryder?" he asked, even though he could guess the answer before the words left this mouth.

She hitched a hand on her hip, and he knew before she said a word that he deserved the attitude she was about to throw at him. "Are you going to try to farm me out to all of your relatives? Besides, I've only met Ryder a few times and he seems a little young for me."

Ryder was a little young for anyone right now. Chase hoped he'd grow up before a bull took him down and he had no future left to live.

She shoved the financial report across the table. "Did you not catch what I'm saying? I'm offering you the money to save the ranch and set up your nonprofit. You won't have to worry about funding anymore."

It was time to get to the heart of this conversation before he came across like a complete jerk.

He took a breath and said more gently, "I apologize, Lexi. But in my defense, this entire conversation feels like a stealth attack."

"Attack?"

"You had to know it was going to catch me off guard."

Leaning over the table, she swept the stapled packets into a pile in front of her. "I apologize for that." She looked at him, her deep brown eyes holding a hint of burden. "I didn't know how to approach the subject. There's not really a manual for this kind of thing."

"How long until your thirty-fifth birthday?"

She took a deep breath and blew it out slowly. "One month," she said softly.

The marriage grenade she'd hurled at the beginning of the conversation spun head over tail toward him. He caught it, pin intact. But if he made one wrong move, it would explode, taking him and his ranch with it. He was wrong. Nothing about getting this money would be easy for Lexi. And he didn't think he was going to be able to help her.

He would have to watch his ranch implode right along with her untouched trust fund.

Lexi saw it in Chase's chiseled face the moment she told him she only had one month until her thirty-fifth birthday.

The defeat of her cause.

The rain picked up again outside, rivulets of water sliding down the tall windows of the great room.

She couldn't let the conversation end. Not until he understood her. "Chase, will you please hear me out?" She held her arm out to one of the leather chairs around the table. "Please. Sit down and give me a few minutes of your time."

After nodding, he folded his military-grade body into the seat across from her, the huge oak table and a massive chunk of tension between them. He crossed his arms over his broad chest for the third time in this conversation. But at least his glare was no longer burning a hole in her resolve. Small victories.

She lifted the stack of papers, neatly placed them on the table and folded her hands on top of the pile.

"I know this sounds ridiculous."

"Illogical," he said.

"Illogical." She cleared her throat. "But it could also be a strategic move to get us both what we want." Thinking about how that might sound to him, she cringed. "Sorry. That's not what I mean. This went more smoothly when I said it to the mirror."

"You practiced in the mirror?"

"Of course I did. This isn't easy," she said, trying to force the insecurity out of her voice.

His face softened, and he leaned across the table and put his hand over hers. "I'm sorry. I'll be quiet."

She raised one eyebrow. Neither of them ever kept their mouth shut if there was an opportunity to give the other one a hard time.

He squeezed her hand and leaned back in his chair with a chagrined look on his face. "Quiet*er*. I'll stay quiet*er*."

"I don't think that's a word, but thanks."

"Lexi, one month out from your birthday, why are you just now looking for a husband?"

She desperately wanted to avoid telling him the embarrassing truth, so she'd start with simple answers and see where that led. "I've known about the trust for a while. I knew it wasn't—" she paused "—probable for me to fulfill the requirements."

His stare remained steady, except for one glint of sympathy. At least she hoped it was sympathy.

"For every trust, there's a trustee. A designated person who verifies the requirements of the trust and dispenses the assets when those requirements are met." He nodded. "The trustee called a few months ago. He was surprised to hear I wasn't married. Shocked, actually."

She ran her thumb over the bottom of her bare ring finger. Not as shocked as she was.

"What happens to the money if you don't get married?" he asked.

"That's just it. For years, it was my understanding that in the event that I wasn't married, the money would simply go to a designated charity. My fail-safe was that if I didn't get married by the allotted time, it wouldn't feel like a total loss. The funds would still go to good use."

"But the phone call changed things." He said it as a statement, not a question.

"Yes. He called to inform me that the trust stipulated that if I didn't fulfill the requirements, the money would go to a second cousin who served some jail time for embezzlement. But in general—" she bored her eyes into his "—he's known for blowing through money as quickly as possible and doing questionable things to get more."

Chase swiped his coffee mug off the table, got up and stomped over to the carafe.

"Isn't that your second cup?" she asked. "You'll be on a tear all day if you have them so close together."

"I'm already on a tear," he said as he poured.

She thumbed the edge of the papers while she waited for the last bit of the conversation to settle. Chase's top always blew when presented with new information, but he was usually quick to adjust if she just waited him out. She only wished that she'd known he'd need more than a month to adjust to her proposal.

He turned around, leaned his hips against the sideboard and crossed his legs at the ankles. Then he zeroed in on her. "Your second cousin doesn't sound like an upstanding citizen. Are you safe?"

Unexpected warmth hit her belly. He always had a protective side to him. Over the last two years, she found herself wishing he would aim it at her more often. "Yes. I'm safe."

"Does he know about the trust?"

"No."

"Well," he exhaled, "there's one less thing to worry about."

"Thank you," she said quietly.

His eyes shot to hers. "Lexi, no matter what has been said between us over the years, I care about you."

"I know. It's why I thought of you." She shrugged and gave him a small smile, one that offered peace. "We might not get along—"

"That's putting it lightly."

"—but I think we have a mutual respect for each other."

He stilled, then nodded.

His agreement gave her the courage to continue. "I've spent the last two years getting to know you and your siblings. People in town think the world of what you've each done to hold your family together. Everyone talks of the strong Cross legacy."

Chase held his head a little higher.

"I know I showed up in your life not long ago. Your family has stories thick with generations of love and loss that I'm not privy to. And you don't often mention your years in the military. But your love for this ranch is written all over you. And when you talk about your vision for veterans who could find restoration on your family's acreage, it's…" She paused to tamp down emotion and beat back the tears. "It's inspiring," she whispered.

Chase said nothing, but his breathing sped up.

"I know it's not conventional. But if you married me, this money could do some powerful things. Otherwise, it's lost forever. My second cousin is sure to squander it in record time."

"You're talking about marriage," he whispered across the room.

"I know."

"There's something I don't get about all of this, and I'm not sure if I'm allowed to ask."

"I think since I suggested that we bind ourselves together for the rest of our lives, you're entitled to a question or two."

He smiled at her for the first time since she arrived this

morning. It was a smile she wouldn't mind seeing the rest of her life, even if she annoyed him so much that he didn't show it often. A smile that spoke of tough living, perseverance and victory on the other side of hard times. A smile that never came easy, but when earned, could stop her in her tracks.

"You said you've known about the trust for a while," he said.

"Yes."

"You're telling me that there's been no candidate to marry you in almost thirty-five years?"

Although Lexi had expected the question, his comment cut into a wound she knew would never heal. "Sometimes a loving marriage just isn't God's plan for everyone."

Confusion crossed his face.

"Before my father died, he taught me about sacrificial love. The key word being sacrifice. God loved us sacrificially. I know you believe that, which is another reason I think we can do this. We both have faith in God, even though it didn't come easy over the years. It might be a sacrifice to actually get married, but it won't be without blessings. If only for the veterans."

He set his cup down and pushed to his feet with an intimidating force. "Lexi, I cannot take away the opportunity for you to marry for real love. That is out of the question."

Panic surged through her body. She was going to have to tell him more, and her heart thundered in warning. She stood up. "I'm not ever going to get married."

He shook his head and took steps around the table to her. "You can let your thirty-fifth birthday pass, let go of the money and wait for the love of your life."

Red spots dotted her vision. He couldn't know the pain he was digging up from her past. "I am. Not. Going. To get married. Ever. You've stated clearly that you wouldn't marry again." Her voice rose, and she didn't care what it said about her desperate state. "Why can't we make this a partnership? Why can't we come together to do something significant for others in need? Why can't we do something honorable with the money?"

Matching her intensity, he said, "Because it's incredibly dishonoring to you."

She threw her arms out wide. "What? Why? I'm walking into this with my eyes wide open."

"I know that. And I want to understand why you're willing to do this. Why you're willing to throw away a chance at marrying for love. Unless—" His eyes crinkled with his smile and his tone changed. "Are you in love with me?"

Years of pent-up frustration bubbled through her veins and came out in ironic laughter. She threw a pen at him, and it bounced off his shoulder. "Are you for real?" She grabbed her stomach and bent at the waist. The pain from the laughter was almost as bad as the pain from the situation at hand.

Lips twitching, he had the decency to look part amused and part guilty. "Okay. So you're *not* in love with me."

Her love life was like a pressure cooker with no valve, heating toward an explosion on her thirty-fifth birthday. But she couldn't get anyone to love her.

And now she couldn't give the money away to save her life.

His noble streak stretched a mile wide. Why couldn't it just shrink this one time?

Her laughter turned to exasperation. "What is wrong with you?"

"I'm asking myself the same thing about you," he shot back.

"If I knew what was wrong with me, I'd—" She stopped.

No. No way was she going to tell Chase the deepest pain in her heart. No way would she tell him that if she knew what was wrong with her, she'd fix it so someone would actually want to marry her because of who she was.

But there was no way around the ugly truth of how she got that wound.

She turned to the windows again and stepped close, ignoring the sad reflection that stared back at her. "I've been engaged twice. Called off weddings. Twice," she said to the glass. It was easier than looking at him, though she heard the small grunt in response.

"Lexi," he said, his voice filled with sympathy.

She closed her eyes, as if that would make the next words easier. "My first fiancé cheated on me with my maid of honor a month before the wedding. My best friend since childhood." The horrid memory of walking in on them kissing flashed through her mind.

He cleared his throat, but remained silent.

"My second fiancé," she said, opening her eyes and turning to look at him, needing him to understand, "sought me out and pursued me because of my grandmother's trust. My mother was part of the matchmaking. I overheard them talking at the rehearsal dinner and I cancelled my wedding the night before the ceremony."

His next response was a growl.

"It's okay. I left town before she could track me down and tell me what percentage of the trust she was going to get for making the match," she went on, even though it wasn't okay. It was, in fact, very not okay. Two years later, the betrayal still pierced her heart, and pain laced the few conversations she'd had with her mother.

Chase placed his hand on her arm, and she stared at it.

"I wish I could fix this for you," he said, his voice gentle. "But I can't do that. I don't want to get married again."

She knew. The death of his wife was too hard on him. She just thought maybe he would view this differently.

"And even if I did," he continued, "I can't marry you for your money. It's just not right."

"Thank you for your consideration of me, Chase." Before he could interrupt her or she could lose her nerve, she continued. "You're a man of integrity through and through. It would have been an honor to marry you. No matter the circumstances."

His only reaction was a slight gape of his mouth.

She shrugged and offered what she hoped was a gracious smile to cover whatever thing was passing between them.

This conversation was a disaster.

Lexi had told herself she at least had to try.

She'd tried. Now she'd disappear from Four Cross Ranch until after her birthday. Maybe forever. She could find Four Cross Ranch another accountant.

He squeezed her arm. "I'll find another way to help the ranch."

"Chase, I just don't know what other options you have."

"If the heifers are doing all right in the morning, I'll head into town. My family has been in these parts for generations. That has to be good for something at the local bank."

Her stomach clenched. She knew he didn't want to have to go down that road.

As he walked out of the room, she realized she shouldn't have chosen someone so honorable to ask to marry her.

She should have called her ex-fiancé.

The one she'd left at the altar because she found out his ulterior motives. The one she knew would definitely marry her for her money.

Yes. She should have contacted Vance Miller.

Chase could go to the bank. But her accounting experience told her that unless he wanted to put the ranch up as collateral, he would get turned down. And with all the problems they'd had in the last year, she wouldn't advise taking that route. They could lose their family's land.

In the meantime, she'd contact a lawyer about the trust. Maybe there was a loophole.

A loophole would solve everything. Everything except the tug in her heart that wished she didn't have to do life alone, that wished Chase had said yes, even if they couldn't always get along.

Chapter Three

Chase had lived a life full of land mines and cow patties, but the situation Lexi had thrown at him yesterday felt more tenuous than either of those.

"What crawled in your cowboy hat?" Chase's twin asked from the passenger seat of the ranch's white F-150 pickup truck.

Chase started the engine. "Nothing."

Clouds dotted the sky. The light grey puffs wouldn't commit to a storm, but they also wouldn't go away and let the sunshine stream over the land.

Hunter picked up the travel mug from the cup holder and stared into the clear, plastic lid. "Have you had two cups of coffee today?"

Shaking his head, Chase headed in the direction of town. It irked him that both his brother and Lexi knew him well enough to know he couldn't handle his coffee. Soldiers and cowboys should be able to drink black tar if they wanted to. "I haven't had two cups of coffee."

"You're in a worse mood now than you were when the cattle crossed the property line last week, and I didn't think that was possible," said Hunter.

Chase didn't think it was possible either until Lexi left him with a parting shot yesterday that could have cleared all the animals out of the barn. After blowing out a long breath, he looked at his brother. "Lexi needs someone to marry her."

Hunter stared out the windshield but said nothing. It was his way. The man had incredible restraint and patience. He could wait out any situation. Chase might as well tell him everything.

After explaining Lexi's ludicrous solution to the problem, he concluded with, "Which is more absurd than the early freeze we had last September."

"Except that freeze actually happened," Hunter said in a sage-like tone.

Chase did a double take. "What's that supposed to mean?"

Hunter shrugged. "I'm just saying the freeze happened."

At the next country road stop sign, Chase threw the car in Park and turned to look at his twin. "Are you implying I should actually consider this? Have you noticed how Lexi and I can't get along for more than five minutes? That's a real problem when you're picking a spouse."

Hunter stared back, his entire body exuding a calm that only ratcheted up Chase's frustration. Of course Hunter said nothing. Silence was Hunter's stealth weapon.

Chase put the car back into Drive, hit the gas and scrubbed a hand over his face. His brother had worn him down quicker than usual, but at this point, Chase would welcome someone else's perspective on the situation. "I didn't sleep last night."

His brother grunted.

"Because I keep thinking about how else she might try to solve this problem. Who else is she willing to marry?" He slammed the palm of his hand on the steering wheel. "She is willing to *marry* someone she doesn't love to get this money."

Another grunt.

"You're right. It's not about the money for her," Chase said on a sigh. "The thought of that cash being squandered away would make anyone sick. I don't even know her cousin and it's a little hard to swallow. And she has a point. That money could be used for good."

Entrance gates to neighboring ranches whizzed by every few miles. Still nothing from his copilot.

Chase pointed his finger to the windshield. "I'll tell you what she needs to do with that money is buy herself a new car. She drives a Civic, no doubt for the good gas mileage, but she has no business trying to maneuver that thing during a Wyoming winter. It's not safe."

Another idea hit Chase. "Maybe it's leftover grief for her grandmother," he said. "Grief does funny things to a person."

They knew this firsthand. The memory of a fistfight between Hunter and their younger brother ran through his mind. He knew not to bring up the subject. The only thing Hunter was more tight-lipped about than a woman he might be interested in was what happened between him and Ryder.

Hunter grunted, but this time he added words. "Why is it, do you think, that she didn't ask me to marry her?"

Something unpleasant bristled up Chase's spine at the thought of his brother marrying Lexi. Something he planned to ignore. "She didn't ask me to marry her. She *told* me I could if I wanted to. There's a big difference."

"Sounds the same to me," Hunter muttered.

The speed limit decreased as they approached town. Chase's thoughts slowed down as well, and he replayed his conversation with Lexi.

"You know what?" he said. "Let's talk about why she

didn't bring the subject up with you. Anything special you want to share with me about your social life?"

"Not that I can think of."

Chase approached the one stoplight in town and signaled his turn onto Main Street. He raised his eyebrows. "Anything about a certain woman in town you've been seeing?"

"Nope." Hunter grinned. "Doesn't sound like anything I want to share."

"Come on, Hunter."

"Sheila." He nodded at Elk Run's Diner up ahead.

"Sheila the waitress?"

He shrugged. "I eat dinner there sometimes. She's nice to me. We go out once in a while."

The men might be opposites, but Chase couldn't picture his twin with Sheila even if she was kind and had a good smile. "Are you interested in her?"

Another shrug. "I like the time I spend with her."

"What does that mean?"

Hunter knocked on the window as they passed the diner. "It means that if we're supposed to be together, it'll all work out."

Angling into a parking space in front of the bank, Chase shook his head. "I cannot wait for the day a woman walks into your life and turns you inside out."

"Kind of like you right about now?"

"You've got to be kidding me." Chase stretched his arm to the back seat and grabbed the manila file folder with the ranch's financials and loan proposition. "Lexi isn't turning my life inside out."

Hunter looked toward the building's glass double doors. "Then why are we going to the bank?"

"I have to find another way to make up for the lost funds at the ranch."

Hunter shook his head as if Chase was missing something. "You're an idiot."

Chase dropped the file folder between them. "Why am I an idiot? For wanting a woman to marry someone for love?"

"Why do you think she asked you?"

Running a hand through his hair, he said, "She said it was because I have integrity. Something about it being an honor to marry me no matter the circumstances."

That finally got a reaction out of his stoic twin. Hunter's eyes grew round. He didn't say anything, of course, but Chase felt like this time was different. As if the words Lexi said had shocked his brother, something Chase had only seen a few times in their lives.

"Plus, I think my dog likes her better than me," Chase muttered.

"Understandable."

He shook his head. "Could you try to be a little more helpful?"

Just then, the Stimpsons strolled down the sidewalk past the truck, their heads together. Mrs. Stimpson laughed at something her husband said to her. When Mr. Stimpson caught sight of the Cross Boys, as the older man called them, he waved.

Chase gave him a thumbs-up to acknowledge the town's most senior and most beloved couple.

What would it be like, just strolling down the street for a lifetime with the woman you love, making her laugh? Once upon a time, he thought he'd get to do that.

Chase had sworn off that kind of life. His anger spewed sideways to Lexi because she'd brought the entire subject up again. A subject he'd declared closed after his wife died.

"What's your biggest concern, Chase?" Hunter asked.

He rubbed his forehead. "What if she marries someone

dishonorable to get access to the money? Someone who doesn't treat her right." Or who didn't appreciate her mad money-saving skills. Or who didn't buy her a safe car to drive. What if she married someone who didn't treasure her?

Hunter's eyes flashed, then he blinked as if to mask the reaction. After years of knowing each other's thoughts before they were spoken, Chase felt annoyed that his twin was so cryptic during this important conversation. "The ranch going under." Hunter counted off the points on his hand. "The money being squandered. Marrying again when you don't want that. Or marrying someone you claim you can't stand. None of those are at the top of your list?"

"No," Chase said, offended, as he angled his body toward his brother. He rested his left forearm on the top of the steering wheel. "I read an article the other day about mail-order brides. I feel sure she can track down a mail-order groom if she were so inclined. That kind of recklessness is much worse than her asking me to marry her."

"You said she didn't ask you."

"She didn't." Chase got out of the truck. "Let's go." He slammed the door and beat Hunter to the sidewalk.

"Interesting that her focus is protecting the ranch, something you're passionate about. And you're intent on protecting her to the point that you're at the bank for a loan. Something you said you would only do as a last resort."

Chase grumbled. There was nothing interesting about any of that. Except the part where he couldn't deny that the words were true.

"You're overthinking this." Hunter opened the tall glass door to First Bank of Elk Run and held it while Chase stomped through.

Chase checked in with a teller, plopped into a worn burgundy leather chair and lowered his voice. "It feels like we're not having the same conversation. Are you even listening to me?"

Hunter raised an eyebrow. "A kind, Christian woman who isn't hard to look at has offered to save the ranch and secure the nonprofit through a partnership that just happens to be sealed with a marriage certificate, but requires absolutely nothing of you. What am I missing?"

He threw his hands up. "I'm not marrying this woman for her money."

"I think the thing you don't understand is that she's not asking you to." He paused. "She's just trying to help."

This time, Chase was the silent one. Was it that simple?

"You guys already fight like an old married couple anyway."

Chase's entire body jolted, and he stared in the wise eyes of the man who knew him better than anyone. Even better than his mother when she was alive.

A picture of his wife, Laura, flashed in his mind. He lowered his voice. "I'm not up for getting married again. You know that."

"I do. I also know that people change their minds."

Across the lobby, a toddler started crying. Chase could not agree more with the kid.

But he couldn't process the warmth that spread through him at the news that he and Lexi already acted like a married couple. Or the visual he had of them walking down the sidewalk. Just like the Stimpsons. He scratched at the left side of his chest, trying to get rid of whatever was happening in his heart.

Chase huffed out a short breath. The army taught him to do his research and plan for all contingencies. "Fine. I'll keep this appointment and get more information about a loan. But saying yes to her is still a possibility."

Hunter studied the mother trying to console her young boy. "Or, you could bypass what is bound to be a rejection by the bank and just go tell Lexi you'll marry her."

"The family would lose their minds," he muttered. Not just his siblings. The ranch hands, too. They were a tight-knit group at Four Cross Ranch.

The little boy toddled over and stood next to Hunter, gnawing on a fist. Tears stained his cheeks, but he was calm, mesmerized by the cowboy in front of him. Hunter pulled the Stetson off his head and placed it on the child, who then giggled. "Or maybe Four Cross Ranch just falls in love with her."

"Exactly." Chase sat back, stretched his legs out and crossed his arms over his chest. When Hunter's words registered, he sat up so quickly, he had to right his hat. "Wait. What? No. I mean, yes. Everyone will like her."

"Everyone will love her." Hunter waved at the kid, but said to Chase, "We still meeting with the banker?"

"Absolutely."

His brother shook his head once. "You really are an idiot."

Walking into the barn, Lexi didn't think she'd ever get used to the smell of horse manure. Really, any manure for that matter. She would take the aroma of her freshly sharpened pencils and office supplies any day of the week.

But there was something pure and honest about the earthy smells of the ranch. Every time she left her house in town and had to go on the property, she was struck by the way the country stripped life down to a beauty that couldn't be duplicated anywhere else. She could breathe here. And she so very much wished Four Cross Ranch could share their space with deserving veterans and their families someday.

But today the only thing she could smell was her discomfort. All the way to the ranch, the knots in her stomach tried to convince her that avoiding Chase would be preferable. But she couldn't avoid him forever. Best to get over seeing him again with something simple.

"I'm an idiot," she murmured to herself.

She walked down the middle of the red horse barn, glancing in each stall for Chase. A grunt sounded from the end of the row.

"Hello?" she called.

Chase stood tall, his mouth tight with a grimace, and rubbed his shoulder. "What?" he barked. When he caught sight of Lexi, he blanched. "Sorry."

Though clearly in pain, the cowboy looked good.

She shouldn't be thinking of him that way. Even if the army-green Four Cross monogrammed shirt set off his well-defined arms and currently blazing hazel eyes. Eyes that held a touch of pain.

A foreign feeling came over her. Was that concern? For Chase? "Are you okay?"

"I'm fine." He bristled. "Do you need something?"

Her fleeting concern for him flew out the barn window. Along with it, her discomfort.

Frayed nerves around Chase? No, thank you. Concern for whatever was bothering him? She would prefer not. But sparring with Chase? This she could do. This was normal.

"As a matter of fact, I do," she said with a little sass. "I need a lot of things, actually. I need the price of gas to go down. And I need someone to create a universal charger for electronics regardless of the device or brand."

He leaned against the handle of the broom. "Apparently, you also need a husband."

His words hit her in the gut, but she pushed through.

"You're aiming below the belt today. Have you had two cups of coffee?"

He closed his eyes and shook his head gruffly. "Sorry. Again." After he blew out a long breath, he looked at her. "I got sent to the barn."

"Hunter put you in the corner for your bad attitude?"

"Something like that. This morning hasn't gone exactly like I had hoped."

"You're going to kill your rotator cuff if you muck stalls all day."

He said nothing, but the muscles in his jaw ticked.

"I'm here because I need your signature on a check for the company who fixed the pipes underneath the chow hall."

"Why didn't you ask Hunter?"

"He's doing fence repair and that would require a horse ride."

"What's wrong with a horse ride?"

"Nothing." Except she'd never been on a horse. "Can you please just sign the check?"

"Can't you just give the company the card?"

"It saves us three percent in fees to write a check instead of using a credit or debit card. Sign this, and I promise I will leave you to your crankiness."

He nodded, pulling off one of his work gloves. "You are on brand, Lexi Gardner. Well done."

"On brand?" she asked as she passed the check and ballpoint pen across the stall gate.

"Consistent. Like you're a brand sold at stores." He held the check against his muscled thigh and waved the pen in a circle with his explanation. "You're always doing things to save the ranch money. Your brand should be Gardner's Savings."

"Gardner's Savings? That's the best marketing slogan

you can come up with?" Giving him the side-eye, she said, "Keep your day job."

Bowing his head, he signed the check, then returned both items back to Lexi. But not without his hand skimming hers. Her eyes shot to his. She snatched the items away, sure that her face was flushed red from the heat she could feel rising up her neck.

What was wrong with her?

He pulled his glove back on and gave her a small smile. "Now I'm going to ask you a serious question."

Her stomach clenched, and she held each muscle in her body still, wary of what was coming.

He placed his hand on the rail and studied her. "Are you doing okay? Really?"

"Yes, fine. Why do you ask?"

"There's that 'fine' again. Which we figured out clearly wasn't true yesterday when you explained your situation to me."

She bit her bottom lip.

"You asked me to marry you yesterday, but you won't make eye contact with me today. What's that about?"

The more she thought about Chase's reaction to her proposal, the more mortification settled into her bones. Her dating history read like a bad TV show. The latest rejection by Chase the crushing series finale.

And it felt final.

She wouldn't get married. Ever. For love or for logic.

She swallowed, straightened her spine and said with confidence, "Well, today, I'm just the ranch's accountant, Chase."

"An accountant who has gone out of her way for her client in spite of an awkward conversation yesterday with one of the owners." He nodded to the check she had personally hand-delivered to his ranch for his signature.

Lexi didn't know why she gave Four Cross Ranch perks. Something felt natural about being on this land and helping this family. She didn't mind completing basic supply orders or contracting work for them.

He gentled his voice. "I'm just checking on you."

What was she supposed to do with his regard for her? It almost sounded like he cared when he'd asked if she was okay.

His mouth curved just slightly, and his eyes looked like he knew something she didn't. "You're so uncomfortable standing there, I think you're considering paying a courier to bring the next check over to be signed even though it would cost you money to do it."

Her lips twitched while she tried to hold back a smile.

"Aha!" He pointed at her. "I'm right."

A horse in the next stall huffed in agreement.

"I appreciate your concern for me, really I do, but I made a phone call that might lead to a solution to my…problem."

Chase narrowed his eyes at her. "What kind of a solution?"

She swallowed, trying to figure out why she was still standing in the barn. "I asked my lawyer to look into the trust and see if he can find any loopholes."

After a beat, he cleared his throat. "Did he have any initial impressions?"

"Actually, he wasn't optimistic. He'll do some research and reach out to a buddy of his who deals with this sort of thing. He's sympathetic, but not optimistic." She sighed and offered a resigned smile. "Then *he* asked me to marry him."

Irritation radiated off Chase. "What?" he growled in a low voice.

"Calm down. He's sixty-three years old. A few years from retirement." A playful smile lifted her lips. "Plus, I think his wife would object to our union."

He pointed at her. "Don't do that to me."

"What?"

"Give me a heart attack."

"What are you so angry about, anyway?"

Chase's golden retriever sauntered into the barn, walking purposefully as if he was mayor of the ranch animals and was here to check on his constituents. When he caught sight of Lexi, his tail wagged double-time and he took off running toward her. She knelt and gave Duke a body rub while she looked at Chase. "I've let you off the hook. This isn't your problem to solve."

"I'm glad you contacted your lawyer. Even if he isn't optimistic." He paused, cocked his head. "Fess up. What did you trade him for his services?"

She shrugged, pleased he would ask. "He had a few questions about his tax return. I spent some time untangling the language for him."

"Lexi's Low-Cost Living," he murmured.

"Seriously?" She stood up. Duke stared at her, his tongue hanging out of his mouth as he panted. "Surely you can come up with something better than that."

His gaze turned concerned. "I hope the lawyer has some good news for you."

There it was again. His protective streak. It felt better than she wanted to admit. But she couldn't lean into that feeling. It was temporary and would only bring her disappointment. "Me, too. It doesn't look good. But me, too."

He opened the stall gate and walked through. When he latched it closed, he glanced at her. He shifted his feet and looked as uncomfortable as she'd felt when she'd arrived this morning. "I think I owe you an apology."

"Yes. You owe me an apology for your appalling marketing slogans. And I accept."

He stared at her, and his jaw muscles clenched. "I'm not sure I've handled this situation well. It seems to bring out the worst in me."

"More than usual?" She hoped giving him a hard time would convince him he was off the hook.

But he shook his head. "You know what I mean."

"I know what you mean." She quieted her voice. "But these aren't normal circumstances. You get all kinds of grace."

He pulled his hat off his head, ran a hand through his hair and studied his Stetson. When he looked up, his stare bored into her, and something worked behind his eyes. "Lexi, what you said yesterday…well, I feel the same way. You're a woman of integrity, too."

Her mouth parted, but no words came out. She didn't know what to say or where this was going, but every nerve ending was on full alert, skittering across her skin as if in warning.

Then his face turned suddenly vulnerable in a way she'd never seen before, as he said, "It would be an honor to marry you."

Her heart hammered. She could feel her chest rising and falling with quickened breaths. It's not that she thought she was going to pass out, but she felt light-headed. Like the world had just tilted a little bit, and somehow she was still standing. Duke rubbed up against her leg as if to steady her, but she could hardly feel the contact.

Chase stepped toward her. "Lexi? You okay?"

She wasn't sure his close proximity helped her inability

to move. She shook her head. Laughter laced with disbe-lief escaped her mouth. "Sorry. I, um. Yes. I—did you just agree to marry me?"

"I believe I did." He twirled his hat once in his hands. "That is, if the offer still stands."

"The offer still stands," she whispered, barely able to speak.

"But I don't think we should do anything rash. I think we should wait until closer to your birthday in case the sit-uation changes." A seriousness crossed his face. "If at any time, Lexi, you want to change your mind, it's okay with me. Do you think that sounds reasonable?"

"I do," she said. "And if at any time, Chase, you want to change your mind, it's also okay. Do you think that sounds reasonable?"

He nodded once. "I do."

In an unusual silence rarely found in a barn, they stared at each other. She took in his features, searching his face for anything that might have looked like doubt or regret. But all she found was confidence and strength. She didn't know what he saw when he looked at her, but she hoped he found evidence of her belief in him and all that he would be able to do with the nonprofit.

The safe haven for veterans would grow and thrive now. And she was so grateful to put the trust money toward something important and significant.

Just then, a bird flew down from the rafters and startled her, breaking the moment between them.

"Well," she said as she tucked a strand of hair behind her ear, "I, um… I need to get going. I've got to change a tire."

He looked out the front of the barn, then back to her. "What happened?"

"Oh, it's just a flat tire." She glanced at her watch and

grimaced in disappointment. She was supposed to make a delivery to the retirement home and then have dinner with the Stimpsons. "I'm afraid I'm going to have to miss my other appointments today."

"Let's go take a look at your tire," he said.

"Oh." She tried to wave him off. "It's okay. I don't want to interrupt your day. I'll figure something out."

"Lexi." He grabbed the hand she was waving and stopped her movement completely. "It's all right. I'll go check it out, and if I need to drive you, then I'll make time to take you where you need to go."

She could feel her brow furrow. "Why would you do that?"

"Because that's what fiancés do," he said, full of logic and void of emotion.

And with that, he took her hand and led her out of the barn as Duke trotted beside them.

Chapter Four

"**I**'m not sure about this," Lexi murmured as the wind blew through her thin red sweater. She wrapped her arms around herself and held on tight.

Clouds covered the sun. Pulling her sweater snug, she was thankful she at least wore jeans. Sometimes, she dressed up to go to Bright Horizons Retirement Community. But today she felt the need to be comfortable. As if the soft fabrics would help her relax during the awkward conversation she wanted to have with Mr. and Mrs. Stimpson.

But what in the world was she going to do with Chase?

The cowboy popped his head up over the trunk of her car. "Are you not sure about my ability to change a flat tire?"

She wasn't sure about having a fiancé. She'd had two and it didn't go well. But this was different, she tried to remind herself. This was just a business transaction.

She didn't need a knight in shining armor riding to her rescue. She was doing just fine on her own, thank you very much.

If only Chase wasn't treating it like he had some kind of duty to perform along with the title, maybe she could calm down.

He raised his eyebrows at her as if waiting for a response.

"I'm not sure I should accept your help. We don't get along. This could be the longest afternoon of our lives."

"Well—" he slammed the trunk "—you don't have a spare, so you're stuck with me. Let's just see if we can get along for more than five minutes."

"And what happens if we can get along for more than five minutes?"

Walking to her, he brushed his dusty hands together. "Then we'll see if we can get along for ten minutes."

Slowly, a smile broke over her face. "Ten minutes would be a record for us. Are you sure we should go in five-minute increments?"

"If we need to set smaller goals we can. But I'll let you handle the numbers part of the process."

"Now you're speaking my language." She smiled, nodding. "That seals the deal. Let's go make each other miserable and see who balks first."

Droplets of rain hit Chase's broad shoulders, but he didn't flinch. She wasn't sure anything could make this man flinch. Other than maybe marrying her, but he was even going to do that.

"Do you even know how to change a tire?" he asked.

"No. But I can follow directions. How hard can it be?"

"Is that how you tackle everything in your life?"

"Sure, if it has instructions."

She'd love an instruction manual on love. Maybe someday she'd have the courage to ask God to explain why she wasn't marriageable material. Gruffly, she shook her head. She had to stop thinking about this kind of thing.

She called the tow truck and tucked the keys on her driver's-side tire. "I can't believe it's so late," she murmured, then turned her focus to Chase. "Are you sure about this?"

"My truck was made in this century. I can take you anywhere you want to go."

"My car was made in this century." She added quietly so he wouldn't hear, "Just not this decade."

His shoulders shook and his next words were said with amusement. "Where can I take you, Lexi?"

"I'm delivering cookies and fresh flowers to Bright Horizons."

Surprise showed in his eyes.

"Don't worry," she said. "I made the cookies from scratch, and I have a deal with the florist."

He cocked his head. "You have a deal with the florist?"

"I buy the flowers that are close to dying at cost." She hitched her thumb to point to the box in the back seat. "I have a slew of vases I got from the granddaughter of a resident at the retirement home. She used them for her wedding, but didn't need twenty vases afterward. Every so often, the florist calls to let me know she has flowers, and I throw them in these vases and take them up to the home."

"You do this all on your own?"

She felt her cheeks heating. "Everyone deserves fresh flowers."

He rubbed a spot over his heart. "Yeah," he murmured, his eyes a thousand miles away. Then he looked at her. "Let's get you and your flowers loaded up in my truck."

When he opened the back door and grabbed the box of floral arrangements, he paused. "What's the rest of this?"

"Casserole dish carriers. I'm also taking a meal to Mr. and Mrs. Stimpson."

After she grabbed the two insulated carriers and reusable grocery bag full of side dishes, they headed to his truck.

He held the box between his body and the truck, opened the back door to the cab and nodded to her to put her things in first. After placing the box on the back seat, he slammed the door and then opened the front passenger side for her. "How do you know the Stimpsons?"

"They were good friends with my grandmother when she lived at the home." Once she was securely inside, he closed the door and went around to his side. Her heart squeezed at his chivalry. Her stomach flipped once. Before he got into the truck, she growled to herself about her new reactions to his kindness and interest in her. Someone needed to remind her body that even though he was now her fiancé, it usually cringed at the first sign of Chase Cross.

"Is this a way to save on gas money?" he asked. "If so, it might be taking Gardner Economics to an extreme."

Her mouth hitched to a small smile, even if she didn't want it to. "Gardner Economics?"

"Yeah. That's my favorite so far. It's not just a marketing slogan. It's an entire way of life."

It was her favorite, too. There was something charming about his brainstorming slogans for her approach to living. But she tamped down the flattery.

He turned the engine on and put the truck in Reverse. "I just saw the Stimpsons in town today." Placing his hand on the back of her headrest, he looked over his shoulder while he backed out, then righted himself and pulled onto the highway.

"What were you doing in town?"

She looked at his profile, his strong jaw working the muscles. "Hunter and I went to the bank to discuss getting a loan," he finally said.

She sat up straight and turned to him, all senses on alert. "What did they say?"

He shook his head once. "They shut me down pretty fast."

"You should've asked me for help. I have all the property financials ready to go."

He threw a smile her way but kept his eyes on the road. "I know. I've kept every last report you've written for the ranch over the last two years."

He kept them? With all the bickering between them over the numbers, she didn't realize he actually valued the work she did for the ranch. She reached over and squeezed his forearm. "I'm sorry they couldn't help, Chase."

The air in the cab changed, almost softened the space between them.

"You really mean that, don't you."

"I do." She released his arm, leaned back in her seat and looked out the window, not seeing anything but his vision for the property. "I believe in everything about Four Cross Ranch. In an odd way, it tethered me to Wyoming when I first moved here, and it won't seem to let go."

With a gentle tone that almost implied he cared, he asked, "Why did you move here, Lexi?"

Ranch land floated by outside the window, green grass dotting the plains with promises of a colorful spring.

"Denver might be a city, but at times it can feel like a small town. After I broke off my second engagement, I needed to get away from everyone and everything. A fresh start." She bit her lip, urging the tears that threatened to fall to go back to where they came from.

Gripping the wheel, his knuckles whitened. "Why Wyoming?"

"My grandmother lived here in Elk Run, and I had some questions for her." She blew out a breath and shook her head. "Why would she leave me a trust with the condition of marriage? Did she realize what kind of strain that would put on me? What that might do to any new relationship I had?" Her voice got louder, the passion behind her questions unleashed. "How was I supposed to go on a first date with someone without feeling unbelievable pressure?"

Chase looked at her, turned his head back to the road, then did an immediate double take, something dawning in his eyes. But he remained silent.

"I had only met her twice in my whole life up to that point. Once I'd arrived in Wyoming, I tried to get my new life started all while dealing with the aftermath of a canceled wedding and an angry mother who was estranged from the woman I was trying to get to know. But before I could get any answers, my grandmother passed away."

The last few miles of the ride, the road rumbled under the tires of his truck as if trying to fill the awkward silence. When he parked the car in the Bright Horizons lot, he turned his body toward her, his face marred with conflict. "I want to ask you something."

She clasped her hands and looked down. "Okay."

"Why is understanding the trust so important to you?"

With one breath, she looked directly into his searching hazel eyes.

"I followed the rules." Her voice was firm. "I went to church. I dated nice men. I made wise choices in those relationships. And look where it got me. Two failed engagements."

His face softening, he stared at her.

Embarrassment crawled up her neck and she felt like it was going to choke her. Why did she blurt all that out to Chase? That was between her and God.

"I had…" she shook her head "…still have questions for my grandmother because it just felt so confusing. Why did she include the marriage condition? What was that going to accomplish? If she wanted to give the money to me, why couldn't she trust me with it as a single woman? Had she thought about the ramifications of the contingency?"

"I don't know."

"I'm sorry," she said quietly. "I didn't mean to get into all of that. I'll just get my things unloaded and you can go."

"Don't be ridiculous. I'll stay and give you a ride home."

"That's okay. I'm having dinner with the Stimpsons." She undid her seat belt. "I was hoping to see if they knew anything about the trust. Maybe get some answers."

Chase looked at the building, tapped his thumb on the steering wheel three times, then aimed his eyes back to her. "Then let's go get you some answers."

For the second time that day, Chase rubbed the spot over his heart. What was that? Tightness? His irritation at the woman in front of him?

If the military taught him anything, it was that rules were important. Sometimes your life or others' lives depended on following well-planned rules. But rules about finding love? That was a stretch, even for him.

Why was it so important to him that she understand she deserved love regardless of a cheating fiancé, confusing trust funds and rules that didn't work the way she thought they would?

In the Bright Horizons community room, he watched as she placed vases filled with colorful flowers on several tables. One woman clutched her hand to her chest in surprise at the sight of the unexpected gift. Lexi meandered through the residents, offering affectionate touches on shoulders, laughing with a few, kneeling on one knee to talk softly to another.

The answer to his question revealed itself. Because Lexi was generous. Kind. Beautiful, if you liked the way her brown eyes lit up when she saw you. Those were just a few reasons it was important to him that she understood she deserved love in her life.

When she finished her floral deliveries, she approached him, and the smile lighting up her face knocked him in the gut. "That was fun," she said.

"It was fun to watch," he murmured, unable to tear his eyes from hers.

A blush hit her cheeks, and she pushed a piece of hair behind her ear. "The Stimpsons are meeting me in their apartment. It's in the independent living wing on the other side of the building."

"Lead the way."

"Chase, I, um…" She looked away and grimaced. Then she said to him, "I would rather not mention to the Stimpsons that we're engaged. Things just feel a little too complicated to tackle that today."

He tipped his hat to her. "I understand."

As they walked, she explained the layout of the facility and how it housed seniors at different stages of life. He remembered her grandmother had moved inside the main building to a lovely room when hospice was needed.

An Easter wreath with a wooden rabbit holding a sign that read "Some bunny loves you" decorated the Stimpsons' door. Mrs. Stimpson answered their knock wearing a sweater adorned with a basket of pastel eggs. Mr. Stimpson stood behind her in a long-sleeved pastel plaid shirt. They wore matching warm smiles aimed at Lexi, then they both were surprised when they caught sight of Chase.

Is that what happened when married couples grew old together? Matching outfits and facial expressions? Chase nodded his greeting to the senior couple.

"Mr. and Mrs. Stimpson, have you met Chase Cross? My car has a flat tire, and he gave me a lift to Bright Horizons."

Mr. Stimpson offered his hand and gave Chase a hearty shake. His wife placed her palm on Chase's cheek. "Of course we know Chase. I changed his diaper plenty of times in the church nursery."

The couple led them into their apartment, then to the dining room. Lexi leaned over and whispered, "I thought you were born a cranky old man."

"I was. They must be thinking of Hunter."

She giggled, and he shook his head. What was he going to do with this woman?

Mrs. Stimpson set out an extra place setting and transferred the food to serving dishes while Mr. Stimpson filled everyone's drink orders.

After they gave thanks to the Lord for the food and fellowship, they filled their plates with Lexi's chicken and rice casserole, bacon-wrapped green beans, and tossed green salad.

"Mr. Stimpson, I don't know how well you know the Cross family," Lexi said while she passed the rolls, "but Chase is a decorated military hero just like you. Twenty years in, four deployments, more honors than anyone can count."

Chase had grabbed the basket but now froze. No one talked about his military service anymore. His parents died when he was twenty-six. Eight years later, he lost his wife. After that, no one noticed his honors or awards, which was fine with him. His siblings had their own lives and challenges. Chase quietly served his last few years and then retired. The focus of the family then switched to creating the nonprofit for veterans. As it should.

Lexi's words of praise felt like a stealth attack that came from his past. Her mention of his service in an overtly proud way gave him pause. Encouraged him even. Which just wasn't something he was used to feeling.

Dinner continued, and for the next twenty minutes Lexi surprised him with her passionate description of the ranch's nonprofit. Mr. Stimpson shared several stories about military buddies who had both struggled and thrived. Between Lexi's enthusiasm, and the veteran's support of the nonprofit, Chase's motivation to get everything up and running was at an all-time high.

"I remember when you and your brother enlisted." Mr. Stimpson dished out a second helping of casserole on his plate. "I'm sure that made your parents proud."

Something unpleasant lodged in Chase's throat. "Thank you, sir. But they probably would have been more proud of Hunter for returning home to take care of our siblings." Would he ever let go of the guilt?

Under the table, Lexi's soft hand slid into his, and he stared from their connection to the sincerity in her eyes. "You were both heroes in your own right," she whispered. She leaned into him a little, their shoulders touched, and she smiled. It was a smile that told him she meant every word.

An unfamiliar warmth spread through his chest. Like something in his insides was thawing after a long winter. Before he could understand what it meant, she squeezed his hand and let go.

Mrs. Stimpson's gaze popped between Chase and Lexi, a glint of mischief in her features. "And how do you two know each other?"

"She's the accountant for Four Cross Ranch."

The woman's eyes glittered. "And what do you think of our Lexi?"

He shifted his weight in the hard wooden chair and felt the heat of the small chandelier lights. It was as if the quaint dining area had morphed into an interrogation room. "I think Lexi can save money in her sleep."

Mrs. Stimpson nodded as if for him to continue.

"If she could make two plus two equal five for her clients, she would."

Mrs. Stimpson lifted an eyebrow, and Chase broke out in a sweat. He wondered if local law enforcement knew about her interrogation skills. If not, they needed to think seriously about employing her.

He rubbed his palms against the tops of his thighs. "What I mean is—" he looked at Lexi and saw a hint of vulnerability in her eyes "—she would do anything she could to help the ranch."

She blinked.

"Anything," he said quietly to her. "And that means a lot to me."

The silence stretched for a few seconds before Mr. Stimpson cleared his throat. He smiled at Lexi. "She certainly is a talented accountant. But everyone around here knows her for her generous heart."

Lexi ducked her head and a blush pinked her cheeks.

"We met her through her grandmother Louella Chadwick. God rest her soul," Mr. Stimpson said with affection.

Chase chuckled. "I got to meet her before she passed. She was quite a pistol."

Lexi placed both palms flat on the table. "Speaking of my gran—" she cleared her throat "—I was wondering if I could ask you two a few questions about her."

"Of course." Concern crossed Mrs. Stimpson's face. "Is everything okay?"

"Yes." Lexi glanced around the table. "If we're all finished eating dinner, maybe we could talk over dessert?"

Mrs. Stimpson shooed everyone to the living room and

scurried off to the kitchen. She returned with a plate of homemade cookies and a stack of napkins. "Lexi, you made my favorite. White chocolate chip without the nuts." She turned to Chase. "Nuts are just nature's way to ruin chocolate."

With her tone as serious as if she were discussing the end-time, he bit back a laugh and nodded. "Yes, ma'am."

She then smiled at him and said, "And we eat our cookies on the couch without a plate. Because I don't have much time left on this earth, and I'm not going to spend it worrying about crumbs. I did that in my twenties, thirties and forties, and I'm not sure it did a whole lot of good for anyone."

While everyone chuckled, Chase wondered if he was going to look back on his life and wonder if he should have approached it differently. His eyes shot to Lexi, and something in his gut stirred.

The Stimpsons settled onto the love seat, Chase and Lexi on chairs that flanked the fireplace.

Instead of holding a cookie, Lexi tightly clasped her hands in her lap. "This might be a bit awkward, but I know you were close with Gran."

"She cheated at bridge," Mr. Stimpson interjected.

"Hush, George," his wife admonished with a stern look.

But Chase couldn't contain his laughter, which earned him the same stern look.

Lexi smiled. "That sounds just like her."

"Go on, sweetie," Mrs. Stimpson encouraged.

"Did she happen to mention anything about a trust fund she left for me?"

Mrs. Stimpson looked at her husband, and he shook his head. "That doesn't sound familiar," she said.

Lexi twisted her fingers one way and then the other. Chase wanted to place his hand on hers to soothe her nerves.

"I know so little about her. We only had those last six weeks of her life together, and I feel like I lost her without really understanding who she was. Did she ever mention anything about marriage or falling in love or money?"

"What's this all about, Lexi?" Mr. Stimpson asked gently.

Watching Lexi struggle, knowing what it meant to her to find answers, filled Chase with discomfort. And the protective side of him wanted to take over the conversation. But why did it feel like he had something at stake in this discussion as well?

Lexi took what looked like a weighted breath. "My grandmother left me a sizable trust fund to be accessed on my thirty-fifth birthday. With one condition. I have to be married."

Mrs. Stimpson's eyes grew round.

Lexi quickly added, "I'm not focused on the money. Even though I've known about the trust and her marriage requirement most of my adult life, I've set myself up to live without it."

Chase watched as she explained about the second cousin who served time for embezzlement. His stomach clenched as she muddled through an explanation of why she wasn't married and how hard it was to find a spouse. And thick guilt hit him head-on when he realized he'd made her this uncomfortable with his recent lines of questioning.

In that moment, her reality hit him like a stampede of livestock. The pressure she felt from her circumstances was underlined with a heartbreaking layer of shame. She'd lived under the weight of a burden she didn't ask for and felt embarrassed by the ridiculous marriage requirement. But she also felt shame because she couldn't find a husband to solve the problem. As if it were a reflection on her.

He didn't like it one bit.

Lexi stood, walked to the window, sighed, then turned back to them. "I just want to know why she would do that. Did she have issues with money or security? Was there a love she lost because of a financial issue?"

At her last question, Mrs. Stimpson's demeanor changed. She pursed her lips and glanced at her husband.

Lexi returned to her seat, leaned forward and rested her elbows on her knees. Her eyes locked onto Mrs. Stimpson, imploring her for an answer. "Did I do something wrong, that she thought she needed to word the trust fund requirements this way? It feels—" her voice became thick, and Chase could hardly stand to watch "—like I'm being punished for something I have no idea I did wrong."

"Now you listen to me, young lady." The elderly woman took Lexi's hands in hers, a fierce look in her eyes. "This has nothing to do with you."

Tears lined the rims of Lexi's eyes, and Mrs. Stimpson continued. "Your grandmother was a fine, upstanding woman. But she was imperfect, like the rest of us. From what she shared with me, her relationship with your mom tested her. She never quite knew how to deal with her daughter-in-law."

"My mother never let me see my grandmother," Lexi whispered.

"I know. And that was one of your grandmother's biggest losses. You need to know that."

Lexi's face filled with a cross between relief and confusion.

"Your grandmother didn't want to speak ill of your mom. But she shared some details with me over the years. Things changed with your mom after your father died. Grief does funny things to people. I don't know what kind of woman your mom was before the accident, but she got it in her head that she needed that money. Your mother did everything she could over the years to get her hands on your grandmother's money. She even tried to declare her unfit."

Lexi gasped, and Chase couldn't handle it any longer. He rose from his chair and stepped behind Lexi, placing a hand on her shoulder.

"Though Louella never talked about the specifics of a trust, she always wanted her money secured tightly, away from your mother." Mrs. Stimpson gentled her voice. "And I think she was a little old-fashioned. She probably wanted you to find someone who could be by your side. And our generation got married earlier in life."

It was so subtle that Chase almost missed it. But everything in Lexi slumped just slightly, almost as if in defeat.

Mrs. Stimpson cupped Lexi's face. "I think if your grandmother knew the pressure she put on you with this trust, she would feel terribly. She loved you. She told me those last few weeks with you were the best of her life. And if she could come back from the grave and change the circumstances of that trust, I believe she would."

Tears streamed down Lexi's cheeks, and Chase felt useless. He squeezed her shoulder.

After somber goodbyes and promises to enjoy a more cheerful dinner another time, Chase and Lexi left. A heavy quiet descended on the car during the drive home. Chase's brain reeled with confusing thoughts. His heart felt even more baffled.

He thought he knew the woman seated next to him. But as they rolled through town under the starlit skies, he realized he'd made more incorrect assumptions about her than he could count.

When they arrived at her house, he walked her to the porch. "Do you need help getting your car back to you?"

She dug through her purse. "No. Thank you, though. The tire shop towed it and said they would get to it tomorrow. They're only a few blocks away, so I'll walk over and get it when they're done."

He felt the edge of his lips tip. "And what will you barter in return for their services?"

"Sometimes I pay people like a normal person."

"Come on," he chided. "Fess up. What is it this time?"

She chuckled, and something tight in his chest released at the sound. "I may have promised to help them unravel their budget issues."

"You are something else, Lexi Gardner." He stared at her sparkling eyes, and everything around them stilled.

She shifted, almost a little bashful, the porch light reflecting off her silky hair. "Thank you for taking me to Bright Horizons."

"It looks like we got along for more than just five-minute increments," he said.

She laughed softly, the smooth sound hanging in the air. "I think that means I need to come out to the ranch and see how it works."

"Why would you do that?"

"Because I'm going to live there and be your wife."

Struck silent, Chase just stood there. The word *wife* played over and over again in his head. He knew he'd agreed to marry her, but somehow talking about it this way made it more real.

She cocked her head to the side. "Will you show me, Chase? Will you show me what my life will be like in a month?"

All he could do was what any good cowboy would do. He tipped his hat and said, "Yes, ma'am."

Warmth hit Chase's chest as he walked to his truck. He could get used to this Lexi.

But as he drove away, he wondered if he wanted to get used to this Lexi.

Chapter Five

"I'm sorry, man," Hunter said through Chase's phone the next evening. "I hate to do this to you. I know Lexi's on her way."

Chase rubbed the back of his neck. "It's okay. It's calving season. If she can't understand what it's like on a cattle ranch during calving season, then we're in trouble."

"She'll understand." Chase thought he could hear a smile behind Hunter's words and decided not to acknowledge it. He wasn't in the mood to be ribbed by his twin tonight.

She had to understand calving season for him the way he had to understand tax season for her. How unfortunate those happened around the same time of year.

Disappointment hung in the air as he looked out over the acreage of Four Cross Ranch. In spite of Wyoming's gorgeous scenery, tonight's sunset seemed dull.

He was hoping to show her the more impressive sides of the ranch on her first visit out as his fiancée. Which irked him because why would he want to impress her? She'd been out here many times before today.

Chase hit the end button for the call and scrolled through his contacts to find Lexi's number. At some point, he supposed he'd have to move her to the Favorites list on his phone. If Hunter had told Chase last week that this week he'd be thinking of moving Lexi Gardner to his Favorites list, he'd have socked him in the arm.

She answered on the first ring.

"Lectured anyone today on the importance of receipt organization?" he asked.

"I may or may not have casually mentioned it to three clients," she said with humor in her voice.

He smiled. "Attagirl." Then he sighed and said, "I hate to do this to you, but I can't greet you at the gate. I'm heading down to the grey barn. We've got a first-time heifer that doesn't understand it's her job to feed her calf. I've got to lend a hand. We should probably cancel the tour and do it another day. I don't know how long this is going to take, and the sun's fading."

"Oh." Chase could hear disappointment in her voice. "Oh, right. Absolutely. I'm sorry. Things at work took a turn and time got away from me."

He lowered his voice. "It's okay, Lexi. Another time."

A long pause filled the call. She cleared her throat. "Is there anything I can do to help?"

He smiled. "I wish you had something to trade this momma to convince her to feed her baby. But I'm not sure if Gardner Economics applies to cattle."

She was still laughing when they disconnected.

Still, he dragged a bad attitude with him into the barn. That spot in his chest ached and it felt a little bit like he was going to miss seeing her, so he did his best to ignore the feeling.

Thirty minutes later, he was grateful no one was around to see him. He found himself shoved to the ground by the momma cow. Grabbing his hat off the floor, he pushed to his feet. Thankfully, the calf had started to nurse. He stroked the momma's back. "Let's be glad you didn't need to be put in the head chute," he said to her. Restraining cattle wasn't Chase's favorite thing, but sometimes it was the only way to get the job done.

"Chase?" a voice whispered from outside the pen. "Are you okay?"

He glanced up and found Lexi, wide-eyed and fidgeting. She looked like a hen who didn't know where to go. Except in her jeans and puffy-sleeved green top, she looked cuter than a hen. "I'm okay now that this heifer is allowing her calf to feed. Are you okay?"

She bit her lip, then released it. "I heard a scuffle back here and thought you might be hurt."

He took off his hat and wiped his brow with the back of his hand. "This is her first calf, and she didn't care for nursing. We had a little chat about it, and I helped her see the error of her ways."

She glanced at the halter the momma had thrown off, and back to him. A smile broke out over her face, but she tried to hide it with a hand. "You're covered in hay."

Hitching a grin, he said, "It may look like I lost the battle, but I won the war." He glanced down at the calf, thankful she had stopped bawling.

"Will the cow know what to do from now on?"

"Sometimes they need a few more bouts of encouragement." He shifted slightly and the heifer gave him a stern look. Calmly, he soothed, "You've got this, momma. You don't need me anymore." At the sight of the heifer nursing, relief hit him. They would be okay.

He sauntered toward Lexi, wiping hay off his staff shirt along the way.

With a face full of wonder, she said, "I can't believe you bring life into the world."

He shook his head. "My sister Cora's the one who has

the superhero midwife powers. I just watch while the cows do what they were born to do. If they need help every now and then, we're available."

"I haven't seen Cora around lately. Does she usually help with calving season?"

While dusting off his jeans, he didn't make eye contact. "She won't set foot on the ranch side of the property."

"Seems like there's a story there."

"There is," he said somberly, shifting his focus back to her. "It's hers to tell. But fair to say that ranch life wasn't good to her."

He was surprised Lexi didn't know what happened to his sister. But maybe she'd been shielded from the rumors.

"I guess Ryder is a no-show for calving season, too?" she asked quietly.

All Chase could do was clench his teeth and nod. If Ryder were here to help, Chase could focus more on the nonprofit.

His rodeo brother was an enigma to him. A riddle he would never solve. But no matter his youngest brother's actions, Chase knew there was a good man in there.

He gave a chin lift to the basket in her hand. "What do you have there?"

Pink hit her cheeks, and she curled a strand of her pretty blond hair around her ear. "Dinner. I couldn't think of a way I could help you with the cows, so I brought dinner."

"That was thoughtful. Thank you."

"It's just a sandwich, chips and carrot sticks."

His shoulders shook with a chuckle. "Carrot sticks?"

"Yes." She spoke with authority. "Everyone needs their vegetables."

He leaned over the edge of the stall railing and lifted the red-and-white-checkered cloth napkin covering the food. "You got dessert in there, too?"

She playfully slapped his hand away. "Only if you eat all your carrots."

He pulled back and laughed.

She looked around the barn and let out a sigh that sounded like contentment. "I like seeing this side of your life."

"I'll always help with the ranch when I can. It's in my blood."

She studied him. "But the nonprofit is your oxygen."

"Yes," he whispered, emotion getting caught in his throat.

"Today's introduction to ranch life got cut short, but at some point, I'd also like to see your plans for the nonprofit," she said.

"You've seen the budget." He pulled hay off his hat. "You already know what I want to do."

"Yes. But I know you have more ideas swirling around in your head about how you want to use your land." She grinned. "Numbers can't show you everything."

He balked. "Don't let your colleagues hear you say that, or you'll get kicked out of Math Club."

She swung the basket back and forth. "I know you mentioned your first guests were coming soon. You're going to eat the cost yourself, aren't you."

"Maybe," he hedged.

"I'd love to help get everything ready. Maybe I could walk the land and see the nonprofit through your eyes and really get a feel for what you need. Will you show it to me?"

How she'd gone from being his biggest critic to his biggest cheerleader, he didn't know.

Maybe he hadn't been fair in his past assessment of her. She wasn't critical of him or his ideas. She just wanted solid foundational funding. She didn't wish for the nonprofit to fail. Which was starting to make him *her* biggest cheerleader.

"Well—" he shifted his hat to his head "—I'd love to do that. But not on foot. That's going to require a horse ride."

"Oh." She stepped back, shaking her head a few times. "Oh, that's okay. No worries."

"It's not a problem."

She looked everywhere but him. "Oh, I don't want to take up any of the ranch's extra time or resources."

He cocked his head and studied her reaction. "Lexi," he said, quiet but firm. She snapped her eyes to his. "What's going on?"

The calf let out a gentle moo behind them, but Chase kept his focus on Lexi.

She pulled on the hem of her shirt. "I kind of…don't exactly…know how to ride a horse."

The words hit him, and a slow grin broke out over his face.

Chase had a new goal in life. One that would take precedence above everything else.

He was going to get Lexi up on a horse.

Four days later, a horse in the stall next to Lexi whinnied.

"What am I doing?" Lexi whispered to the horse. She wasn't sure if she was more nervous about riding, or about spending more time with Chase. Whatever the case, here she was about to hop on a twelve-hundred-pound animal.

She stared at the beautiful light chestnut horse named Mildred, who Chase assured her was as calm as her name. He'd reverently brushed a hand down her side and said she was the most loving animal on the ranch.

Chase had headed to the tack room and left Lexi with the quarter horse. Having been in Wyoming two years, she knew enough to wear jeans and boots. But my word, she felt out of her element. Even though somehow, the ranch brought her peace like it always did.

She wished that peace would line up with her feelings about its owner. In a bizarre turn of events, she seemed to be enjoying him. She'd spent pockets of time over the last few days learning the ropes of the ranch while bringing small items to the lodge for the upcoming guests.

The horse stepped closer.

"Feelings aren't a part of a business proposal, old girl." Lexi ran her palm over Mildred's neck.

The horse adjusted her tongue around the bit in her mouth.

"You really pulled the short stick on names, didn't you? Mildred. That's not how I would describe you."

Chase chuckled from behind her, hoisting a saddle on the wooden rail. "Don't knock the name. It helps first-timers feel comfortable."

He brought the sixteen-hand horse out of her stall, murmuring soft words to her as he led her into the open air of the paddock. After he tied off Mildred's rope, he fetched the saddle.

While he worked, she studied him.

Chase had so many dimensions to him, she'd stopped counting a long time ago. She found the role of sensitive cowboy more attractive than she wanted to admit.

He pulled at the saddle buckle under Mildred's belly and made adjustments. The creak and smell of the leather grounded her to the heartbeat of the ranch.

"So, what's behind her name?"

"Mildred means gentle strength." He ran a hand down her leg. Mildred's shiny light brown coat turned to a stunning black just above the knee in a beautiful contrast that matched her mane and tail. "Which is perfect for her because she really is the most intuitively gentle animal on the ranch. She's going to follow my lead, just like she will with the kids who visit the lodge."

"And her strength?"

He stood to his full height, impressive in his jeans, boots and Western shirt that tugged subtly at his arms and broad chest. "Millie's also the most protective animal on this ranch. She'd never let anything harm you."

Chase seared his eyes into Lexi's, and she knew, even though he didn't say the words himself, that he also would never let anything harm her.

Suddenly, the death of his wife hit her from a different angle. It wasn't just that he'd lost his wife. It was that he lost her to something he couldn't protect her from.

No wonder the soldier didn't want to get married again. Laura's death had wrapped its tentacles around Chase's most vulnerable point and squeezed.

Lexi took a breath and released as much tension out of her muscles as she could. The best way she knew how to show Chase that he could relax and enjoy himself was for her to lead the way. "Okay, cowboy." She cocked a smile at him. "Let's get me in this saddle, and you show me your land."

His lips twitched. "Yes, ma'am."

She walked up to the horse, which brought her closer to Chase. He smelled of earth, and maybe a little bit of hope.

"Left hand on the saddle horn. Put your left foot in the stirrup, push up and swing the other one on over."

Lexi followed the directions and when she hiked her foot into the stirrup and whipped her opposite leg around the saddle, she was surprised at how natural it felt.

"Mildred is the perfect size for you," he murmured while

he adjusted the stirrups. After handing her the reins, he said, "Wait until you see Harvey."

"Harvey? Where do you guys get these names?"

Chase jogged back and then led his horse out of the barn.

Lexi felt her eyes widen at the sight of the black Friesian. "Whoa. Harvey's huge."

"About three hundred more pounds than Mildred." He guided Harvey toward Lexi. After mounting, he leaned over and released Mildred's rope from the fence.

As Chase took the lead, Mildred fell in line behind him. The movement of the horse underneath Lexi felt clunky, but not scary. She loosened her grip on the saddle horn.

"Mildred and Harvey." She chuckled, and Chase looked back at her. "They sound like an old married couple. Mildred and Harvey."

Chase patted Harvey on his neck. "Don't listen to her, buddy. She doesn't know."

"I don't know what?"

"Harvey means battleworthy."

Mildred. Gentle strength. Harvey. Battleworthy.

With acres of grass crunching under the horses' hooves, the sun lowering in the sky and a light breeze swirling around them, a soft peace fell over Lexi. Gentle strength and battleworthy felt about right.

An hour later, they sat on their horses at the tree line on the back edge of the property, looking out over the land that would someday be the playing ground for Four Cross Hope. Guests would stay at the lodge for now, but he had plans for expansion.

"How do you feel on that horse?" he asked. "Because it looks like it comes naturally to you."

"Pretty good, actually. Mildred makes this easy."

"So, I showed you where the individual tiny cabins will be built. But look across this meadow." Chase pointed to Hunter in the distance working with a small dog. Beside them, Duke stood alert as if he were supervising the entire lesson. "That's where the play and therapeutic area will be."

Lexi looked around, the complete picture becoming clear. "That's perfect because the trails will lead here."

"Yeah," Chase said, leaning his weight into his hands at his saddle horn. A simple word, but laced with pride.

"Chase, this is so well planned. Each of the ten houses has a private trail that leads to and from the community areas. Every path points to the chow hall and recreation spots, but there's enough open land that if someone didn't want to get pigeonholed anywhere, they could just breathe in the space."

She swallowed, unsure if she should say what she was thinking, then gentled her voice. "You laid the main features out between the trails like the runs on a ski slope." She paused. "It's like you brought a piece of Laura here."

Slowly, he turned to look at her. He cleared his throat, but didn't say anything. Instead, he took her hand in his, squeezed and looked back across the property.

He didn't let go of her hand, and the moment filled with warmth.

Closing her eyes, she took a long breath in and allowed the exhale to take its time on the way out.

But Mildred shifted her footing and jerked her head up once, yanking Lexi's attention to the horse. Lexi tore her hand from Chase's and grabbed the reins at the ready. Up until now, Mildred had done nothing out of the ordinary. The horse just followed in step with Chase.

"Whoa, girl," Chase soothed, and leaned over to run a hand down her horse's neck. Mildred shook her head back and forth as if she were shaking off a bad thought, then she lowered her head and stomped on the grass.

From afar, Hunter waved.

Lexi lifted her hand in response. "Hunter's going to train the therapy dogs himself?"

"He worked with a K-9 unit in the military, so that's the goal. But his service was so long ago, he's got to go through certification, and that takes resources. In the meantime, I've got a buddy I know who owns a training facility for service dogs. I'm hoping to consult with him."

"Have you thought about equine therapy?"

He nodded. "Another goal. We've got the land out here to make that happen. I've done some general research, but it would take more manpower and funding."

"You never know. You might find a therapist with a horse that needs boarding and make some kind of a deal."

A grin slowly spread across his face, and he cocked an eyebrow at her.

Her shoulders shook with her giggle. "Don't say it. I know. Gardner Economics."

He nodded, the grin still intact.

"But it works," she insisted, sitting taller in her saddle.

"And what did you trade for your new, fancy boots?"

Heat hit her face. She didn't think he'd noticed her shiny new Western boots. "Well…" The wind pulled at a lock of hair, and she tucked it behind her ear. The lock came loose a second later. "If you must know," she said defensively, "I paid full price for these boots."

His gaze shot from her boots to her eyes. "You paid full price?" he asked quietly.

"If I'm going to be living on the ranch, I thought quality was important," she said just as quietly.

The long-term implications fell between them. Lexi's

heart sped up. Maybe Chase's thoughts weren't going in the same direction hers seemed to be galloping.

But his face softened, something so beautiful, it made her heart shift. He leaned toward her and pushed the errant strand of hair behind her ear. "You made a good choice," he said, his voice low and gravelly.

Lexi didn't know what to think about the thick emotion he held in his voice.

But Mildred jerked her head again. This time adding an anxiety-riddled whinny to her movement.

Chase reached for Mildred's bridle, but Harvey reared up on his back legs.

With no time to think or digest what was happening, Lexi gripped the saddle horn. Panic hit her with the next jerk of the horse when Lexi realized she had dropped the reins.

Mildred backed up, her front feet pushing against the hard ground in a way that lowered Lexi forward in the saddle, then jerked her up over and over again. The horse twisted and bumped against Harvey, pushing the other horse forward. The startled Harvey thrust his head up and down in protest and stomped his front legs several times.

"Snake," Chase growled loudly, trying to gain control of his bucking horse. Harvey stopped trying to throw Chase, but pounded his hooves to the ground in his disapproval.

Snake.

Fear slapped her in the face. Every muscle in her body clenched tighter to her horse.

Chase turned his animal away from Lexi, took him several feet in the opposite direction, threw his leg over the saddle and slid off. He hit his horse on the rump, sending him across the pasture on a run.

The sound of Duke barking grew closer, but Lexi

couldn't process what that meant as Mildred started to buck in small jumps that lifted Lexi out of the saddle. On one of the downward motions, Lexi's left ankle got caught at an odd angle in the stirrup, and her knee twisted. Pain shot down her leg and made it difficult for her to maintain her tenuous grip on the saddle horn.

"Hang on, Lexi." Chase tried to grab Mildred's bridle, but it slipped from his hands. "Come on, old girl. It's okay," he grunted while shifting between the horse and the snake.

After vaulting over a log to get to them, Duke skidded to a halt five feet from the snake.

Chase's face tightened. "Duke, back up," he said gruffly, finally able to get his hands on the bridle.

The dog snapped furiously at the snake. The reptile rose taller and hissed a ferocious reply.

"Chase," Lexi breathed out, squinching her eyes at the pain in her knee.

"I've got you," Chase soothed.

Lexi was unsure if he was talking to her or the horse, but his words seemed to calm both of them.

Duke and the snake continued to duel. The snake slithered back a foot, but kept its eyes on Duke and let out an eerie hiss. He'd launch forward six inches, only for Duke to snarl, and in turn he'd slink backward.

Mildred stomped her front hooves, but her overall demeanor calmed down enough for Chase to lead her several feet away from the canine–reptile dance.

Chase smoothed his hand down the horse's neck. "You're okay, girl. You're okay."

Lexi glanced at Duke. The dog had sent the snake cowering back to the forest. He sat on his hind feet, chest puffed out, eyes alert on the trees in front of him. If the last few minutes hadn't been so intense, Lexi would have laughed at the canine mayor of Four Cross Ranch kicking some-one out of his town.

Chase wrapped his hand around Lexi's calf. "Can you take your feet out of the stirrups? Let's get you down on solid ground."

The second she tried to move her left leg, pain slammed into her knee. "Hold up," she gritted through her teeth.

Alarm shot through Chase's features. "What's wrong? Are you hurt?"

"I wrenched my knee."

With deft movements, Chase lowered the stirrup so she could ease her foot from its hold. "Is your other foot out?"

She nodded.

He wrapped his arm around Lexi's waist and slowly guided her off the saddle. It was not one of Lexi's more graceful moments in life, but Chase didn't seem to care.

In fact, Lexi noticed that Chase seemed to be in his own world. Sweat lined his shirt, and his face remained locked with intensity.

Mildred's shoulders twitched, and she huffed out a neigh, appearing to shake off the same stress Chase and Lexi were trying to recover from.

"I think from now on, I'm going to call her Millie," Lexi said, her voice shaky despite trying to lighten the mood. "She's too strong to be a Mildred."

With a fierce look behind his eyes, he gently grasped her hands and rubbed his thumbs across the tops. "Are you okay? What hurts?"

"Just my knee," she said quietly.

One of his arms slid around Lexi's shoulders and pulled her to him; the other one wrapped around her waist. "I'm sorry, Lexi. I'm so sorry."

She clung to him and tried to get her breath under control. Part of her wanted to stay in the cocoon of everything that was Chase Cross, his strong arms, earthy smell and everything that made her feel protected. But another part of her knew his reaction felt a little off.

Something had shifted in Chase. He went from hero in a harrowing situation to someone being consumed by an overwhelming concern. While the sentiment felt good on the surface, she couldn't pinpoint what was happening. It was as if he was drenched in worry for her.

"Chase," she said gently. She pulled back from him, gripping his strong forearms for balance. "Chase, I'm okay."

He ran a hand over his mouth, but kept the other one available for her to use for balance. "I thought…" He shook his head. "Something really bad could have happened to you."

The picture that hung in the great room at the lodge of Laura skiing down one of her last black diamond runs came to Lexi's mind.

And when Lexi realized what was happening, her heart broke.

He was scared for her. Chase didn't want anything to harm Lexi.

She wouldn't allow anything to harm him as well. She had to let him know that everything turned out fine.

"Hey." She pointed to her knee. "I just need to walk this off. It's okay."

She didn't know if it was really okay. She just hoped so for his sake.

"And…" Lexi swallowed and lightened her tone. "You were right about Millie. Gentle strength. She *is* the most protective animal on the ranch. No way was she going to let that mean snake get anywhere near me."

Chase grabbed the back of his neck and looked around,

as if replaying the incident in his head. Though he wasn't looking at Lexi, he gave a small nod.

"Plus—" Lexi ran her thumb over his arm "—Duke came to save me."

His attention turned to his dog.

Lexi said in a playful tone, "I don't want to cause any strife between you and your dog, but I think he likes me more than he likes you."

Chase turned his head to look down at her. He studied her face and sighed. "That's probably true."

"Chase. I'm all right. Promise."

Hunter arrived driving a small ATV. After he studied the scene, he said, "I think I missed all the fun."

"Lexi's hurt," Chase said.

"I'm not hurt." She shifted her glare from Chase to Hunter. When Chase's back was to her, she bugged out her eyes at Hunter, willing him to size up the unspoken pieces of the incident. Surely Hunter knew that Chase needed to believe Lexi was okay.

Walking over to Millie, Hunter pulled a few pieces of apple out of his pocket. He held them out for the horse, who gobbled them out of his hand. "Was it a snake?" he asked them while studying Millie.

Chase walked to the edge of the tree line. "Yes. But I didn't get a chance to see what kind."

"She just remembers being bit." Hunter stroked his hand down Millie's head, placating the horse even further. "I'm sorry, girl. That wasn't much fun the last time, was it? You didn't want Lexi to experience that, did you?"

While the men were distracted, Lexi stretched out her knee. She bit back the moan, but couldn't help the wince on her face.

Hunter's eyes shot to hers.

She held out her hand and shook her head, imploring him not to tell Chase. "I'm fine," she whispered as she put weight onto the knee to show him how fine she was. Only she wasn't fine. Her knee screamed at her. But she knew if she walked a little bit, it would find its bearings.

Chase bent to Duke, giving his loyal dog body rubs and praises for his valiant effort to scare the snake away.

Meanwhile, Lexi hobbled to the other side of Millie, trying to hide her limp from Chase. A few steps later, and she was right. Her knee ironed out the kinks, and she only felt a little soreness. Instead of screaming at her, her knee seemed to be gently admonishing her on the perils of horseback riding.

But she was tough. She could take it. And Chase wouldn't need to know. He didn't need that kind of pressure after losing his wife.

Hunter adjusted the stirrups on Millie's saddle. "I'll take Mildred and round up Harvey. He's probably at his favorite watering hole. You can ride the ATV back to the lodge." With a wave, he trotted across the prairie with Duke at his side.

Lexi had almost forgotten about Harvey. Once she and Chase were settled in the ATV, she asked, "Why did you send Harvey away?"

Chase turned the vehicle around and pointed it to the lodge. "He gets a little aggressive sometimes under stress. I knew if he saw the snake or if I needed to calm Millie down, he wasn't going to be any help."

"Battleworthy," she said. "True to his name." And to his owner.

Before Chase hit the gas pedal, he leaned his weight into his folded arms over the steering wheel and looked at her with an apology in his eyes. "I think I ruined our outing.

For sure I ruined our dinner. Harvey ran off with our food in his saddlebags."

"You didn't ruin anything." She offered him a small smile and shifted her attention to the acreage in front of them. "I've loved every second of getting to know your land, your dreams."

Chase took her hand in his. She wasn't sure if it was his hand trembling or hers, but the connection seemed to calm her adrenaline down.

"Can I ask you a question?" he said in a low voice while staring at their joined hands.

"Yes."

"Is this land, these plans—" he released her and ran his hand through his hair, a stark look of vulnerability in his eyes "—are they worthy of you giving up marrying for love?"

If he was going to risk asking the question, she would risk answering it honestly. She took his hand back.

"Growing up, I think I always knew that my mom was a difficult person to get along with." She sighed a long and heavy breath full of years of frustration, misunderstanding and confusion. "But there's nothing like the moment when you realize that your mother is just a selfish person. It's hard to reconcile that."

Chase used his thumb to rub lines from her wrist to each of her knuckles, and his eyes remained focused on her hand.

"But my dad raised me different. I think he knew he'd have to balance her out." She shook her head, remembering her father's constant attempts to cover up her mother's actions. "But I was wired like him. We were two peas in a pod. I think he knew I'd be okay."

Chase shot his gaze to hers but said nothing.

"I always knew the trust existed. But when I found out

my mother had handpicked a husband for me and set up my entire relationship to her advantage, something broke in me." Her voice cracked, and she whispered, "I knew I had to do something beautiful with that money. To make it mean something."

"Lexi—"

She pulled their hands to her and squeezed, her voice begging him to understand. "It has to mean something, Chase. It has to go toward something good."

His eyes sharpened. "That's why you're willing to forgo love and marry someone?"

"Yes," she whispered.

"Why me?" he asked gruffly, as if trying to contain emotion.

So low, she was barely able to hear her own voice, she said, "Because what you can do to help veterans here is truly beautiful."

He swallowed, his Adam's apple bobbing.

After a beat, he said, "You're an exceptional woman, Lexi Gardner." He lifted her hand and kissed the back of it, his lips lingering just a touch. "I don't think I could have survived if something had happened to you today."

For most people, that sentiment would have spoken of sweet affection. But with Chase's burdened tone and his tortured past, Lexi's heart beat with pangs of confusion.

The table had turned.

In the beginning, Chase didn't want her to marry someone who didn't treasure her. But now, she didn't want him to marry her if he truly didn't want to get married again. Maybe his wounds from the death of his wife were imprinted too deeply. Maybe she was asking too much of him.

But he'd said yes, and she had to trust him. Clearly, if he

had agreed to get married again, it was for function only, which is the way she wanted the deal.

So, it was time to forge forward.

She squeezed his hand, let it go and brightened her voice to transition them out of the jarring snake incident. "The good news is, nothing happened to me today. That leaves me to share my big find for the guest room at the lodge. Which, I might add, is just in time for the Forresters' arrival tomorrow, and as a sidenote, I worked it out so I could be available to welcome the family with you."

"Oh, good. Thank you for arranging to be here." He rubbed his hands together, playing along. "Okay. I can't wait to hear about your big find. But if you paid a penny more than fifty percent off whatever this item is, I'm going to be disappointed in you."

She blanched. "Chase Cross, that's just insulting. I'll have you know I got this particular item for three dollars."

"Which is…"

"A throw pillow that says 'Cowboy Rule Number One: Don't Jog with Your Spurs On.'" She giggled so hard, she barely got the words out.

On a groan, he said, "Lexi, that's terrible."

She laughed harder. "It's hilarious."

"It's terrible."

"Well, let's wait until tomorrow and let the Forresters be the judge."

As they drove to the lodge, it felt good to laugh with Chase. But Lexi was still worried about what the future would bring.

Chapter Six

Lexi could not believe this was happening. She'd had to put out so many fires today with her accounting clients, she'd missed meeting the Forresters at the lodge. Chase said it went well, but she was still disappointed she wasn't there to meet the first military couple to visit Four Cross Hope.

Late afternoon, she had texted Chase to let him know she was finally on her way. He was busy with a heifer in labor and asked if she could sign for a fertilizer delivery. Signing a document seemed more up her alley than delivering a calf. But she couldn't have imagined how wrong the fertilizer delivery would go.

Wiping sweat off her forehead, she grimaced. She was pretty sure her makeup was melting off her face. And she felt positive that the rolls of long, soft curls of hair she'd worked so hard on had flattened to her head.

She looked at the Four Cross Ranch foreman, his weathered face flushed with color. "Frank, I think we've got the last box of fertilizer back on the loading dock."

"Yes, ma'am."

It's not like she dressed up to see Chase. All she did was pair a nice shirt with her best jeans. Though she now worried about sweating in the stretchy crepe jersey top. She didn't want to change because she thought the Swiss dots on the puff sleeves added a delicate touch. Something feminine to her usually uber-practical wardrobe. And so what if she put on makeup and spent time on her hair?

Wait.

What was she thinking? He was supposed to marry her. Not date her.

Then why—on a regular old Monday—did her heart flutter in ways she wished she could cut off at the knees?

She didn't need any feelings confusing her. If Chase wanted to marry her, it was for the money. Which was fine. Because that's what she proposed. Right?

"Lexi?" Chase stood at the bottom of the cement steps. A booted foot with faded jeans rested on the second step. One hand on the metal railing. Her gaze followed the sleeves of his starched long-sleeved navy shirt to find his freshly shaven, perplexed face.

"You look nice," she blurted, then covered her mouth in horror that she'd said the words out loud.

"Calving season's not always glamorous. I had to shower and change." He grinned. "You should have seen me half an hour ago. We for sure wouldn't have gotten along for ten minutes."

"And the clean shave?"

He scratched the side of his cheek. "I'm hoping for fifteen minutes, so I went fancy."

She laughed.

Behind her, Frank cleared his throat. She whirled around. "Frank. Thank you so much for your help. Again, I apologize for the mix-up."

Frank crossed his arms. "We still have a problem," he said, irritation in his tone. Chase looked at Frank, and Frank explained. "The fertilizer order got messed up." His eyes slid to Lexi.

"I know. I apologize. I—" she stammered "—I will fix this."

"By tomorrow morning?" Frank asked, his tone insinuating that he clearly didn't think she could. "We hired extra hands to help us get the fertilizer in. If we don't stay on schedule, it will decrease our hay production. Time is not on our side."

She couldn't blame him for his frustration. She had no idea how to solve this. "No. I can't get a delivery tomorrow."

Chase looked at her. "Is this the—"

"Yes." She sighed and closed her eyes. A second later she found her courage and looked directly at him. "This is the cheaper fertilizer company you warned me about. The one you said was poorly run."

To his credit, his face remained relatively blank, but something worked behind his eyes. They stared each other down, Lexi bracing for the reprimand she knew was coming, Chase probably calculating just how quickly he could fire her and cancel their marriage agreement.

Instead, he surprised her with his calm demeanor. "How soon until the new order comes in?"

"Next week." She didn't know much about farming the land, but she knew if her decision to save on fertilizer caused problems with their hay production, they would have to supplement with feed for the cattle. An unexpected budget item.

He pulled his phone out of his back pocket and sent a text. While they waited, he looked at her and winked.

Lexi stood frozen, trying to ignore the butterflies in her belly. My, he was handsome.

But the wink was different. Some men winked so often that it was part of their vocabulary. But not Chase. She'd never seen him do this before, and the gesture was something personal between the two of them as if it were their secret language.

No. She was not going to be able to ignore the fluttering in her belly.

A soft ping alerted Chase to a response. He looked at the screen, nodded and shot off a second text. When he slid his phone back into his pocket, he said, "Thank you, Frank, for your help. The Hendersons have enough fertilizer to help us out the next few days. We won't miss a beat. I'll head out and bring it back up here."

"You want me to do it, boss?" Frank asked.

"No. You're already working on your day off." Chase looked out over the property. "You've got to pace yourself during calving season. Go grab yourself some grub from the chow hall before your next round to check on the cattle."

Once Frank said his goodbye, Lexi clasped her hands and looked at Chase. "I guess I botched your dinner."

Chase raised his eyebrows. "Why is that?"

"Well—" she shifted from one foot to the other "—you're going to have to get the fertilizer."

"Yes. Which has just become Phase One of your Official Four Cross Ranch Orientation." The side of his mouth hitched in a small grin, and he cocked his elbow and offered it to her.

She couldn't help the giggle that bubbled out of her. She eyed him, then tentatively hooked her arm through his. "Phase One, huh?"

"Yes, ma'am." He led them toward the parking lot.

"Even though I used the fertilizer company you warned me about?"

He stopped. The look on his face caught her off guard. His hazel eyes turned serious. Sincere. "I'm starting to understand, Lexi, that our disagreements about budget items aren't because you don't understand ranch life or that you want to argue for the sake of winning a debate. But because you really want what's best for our property."

"I want you to get what you want, Chase," she said quietly. "I want Four Cross Hope up and fully functional."

He studied her. "I know."

Once they started walking again, she asked, "Did my fertilizer mistake ruin our ten-minute streak of getting along?"

A muscle in his cheek twitched and a glint of humor hit his eyes. "Not at all. The ten minutes hasn't technically started yet."

A soft breeze crossed their path. She wasn't sure what was happening, but something was shifting ever so slightly with the two of them. "Well, that's good. Because after hauling all of that fertilizer, I think I smell like a barn."

"You smell like the outdoors," he said in a low voice, "with a touch of wildflower."

Her belly fluttered again, and she shook her head. "Yesterday went well. Today, you're complimenting me. I'm not sure how to act if we're actually going to get along."

"If it gets too awkward, I can strike up an argument to put us both at ease."

She chuckled. "Listen, I'm sorry I wasn't here to meet the Forresters."

"It's okay. They got settled in. You'll get to meet them later." He veered them toward the ranch company truck and opened the passenger door for her. "How did work go for you today?"

"I might have picked up my phone to make a call and instead of putting the phone number into the phone app, I tapped it into the calculator app."

Chase threw his head back and laughed. It was hearty

and full. And for just a few seconds, she got caught in the beauty of it.

Flutters again. Maybe she just needed to stop looking at him altogether.

After opening the door for her, he walked around the truck, hopped in and secured his seat belt. He turned on the ignition and threw his arm around the back of the seat to look behind them, his fingers grazing her hair in the process. But he froze, his attention caught on something at Lexi's feet.

When she looked down, she gasped. She'd completely forgotten she'd shoved her jeans into her boots and pulled her socks over them and up to her knees. "I'm so embarrassed," she murmured. "I was trying not to get my jeans dusty when we were hauling in the delivery. I stretched my socks over them as far as they'd go." Not knowing if she'd have time to change, she'd tried to preserve her jeans, even if she had to sacrifice her favorite socks.

She reached down to her boots, but Chase stopped her hand.

"Do your socks have a message written on them?" he asked.

She grinned, pulled the boot off her foot and angled her calf so he could see.

He read the words out loud. "'You are courageous.'"

Quickly, she pulled her jeans out of her sock, yanked the boot back on and straightened her jeans over the boot. She repeated the process for the other foot, feeling ridiculous.

He placed a hand on her arm, a playful tone in his voice. "Do all your socks have messages on them?"

"Maybe."

A small smile ticked at the sides of his mouth as he threw the truck in Reverse. While backing out, he said, "I need to know what your other socks say."

She giggled. "Why?"

"I don't know." With humor in his voice, he turned onto the country road. "All of a sudden, finding out your sock secrets has become a priority in my life."

"We'll just have to see how it goes for you."

Eight flats of fertilizer later, Chase and Lexi returned to the ranch and drove down to the storage barn.

"How can I help?" Lexi asked, looking at the giant fertilizer bags. No way she could lift one of those on her own.

Chase hefted one of the bags over his shoulder. "You can tell me what yesterday's socks said."

She crossed her arms in feigned defense. "Nice try."

"I'll take care of this. Why don't you go down to the chow hall and grab some dinner. I'll be there shortly."

With a nod, she turned on her boot and headed across the ranch. When she arrived at the door to the chow hall, her phone buzzed with an incoming text. It was from Chase.

Nate Forrester called. Problem with the master suite toilet leaking at the lodge. I want to fix it while they're out to dinner. I'll finish up here, check out the problem at the lodge, then head to the chow hall.

She immediately texted him back.

No worries. I'll go look at the toilet.

Three dots showed on her phone, indicating he was replying, but she shoved her phone in her back pocket before he could send a response. She was already on her way. She could fix a toilet with the best of them.

The xeriscape plants on the porch of the lodge tied the building to the surrounding fields. Instead of looking out of place on the beautiful land, the wood-and-stone house appeared to grow from the valley itself, as if a haven. A secret shelter at the foot of the mountains.

After grabbing a plunger and a toolbox from the maintenance closet, Lexi headed to the problem.

In the bathroom, Lexi was assessing the situation when her phone pinged with an incoming text that she ignored. She pulled a wrench out of the red metal box and got to work.

Moments later, Chase entered the master suite and approached the en suite bathroom. "You're working on the toilet? I texted and told you I'd handle it." His surprised and almost exasperated tone threw her off guard.

She turned to him and used the back of her wrist to edge a lock of hair off her forehead. "I can do it."

He stood in the door frame, hands splayed on his hips, face perplexed. "I figured you for a call-the-plumber type."

She arched an eyebrow at him.

"Never mind." He swiped a hand through the air as if to erase his statement. "Gardner Economics would never let you hire someone to solve something you already know how to do."

"Plus, these pipes are new. I just figured the problem would be simple to fix. All I had to do was turn the wrench a few times to tighten the joint."

He shook his head as if her answer wasn't good enough. "But why would you volunteer? This is not a pleasant job."

Taking a moment to gather her thoughts, she washed her hands and dried them. She turned to him, crossed her arms over her chest and leaned a hip into the sink counter. "Chase. This is your life. It's also about to be mine. I want to help."

His eyes softened, and the room fell silent for a few seconds. Finally, he took a breath and nodded. "Okay. I get it."

"You do?"

"Yes." He scrubbed a hand down his face. "But I'm still worried about something."

"What's that?"

"So far, Phase One of Four Cross Ranch Orientation has involved a lot of manual labor." A sparkle hit his eyes. "I've got to up my game."

She giggled and shook her head. "You're original, I'll give you that."

"Hand me the plunger and toolbox and then we'll head out for dinner at the chow hall."

They exited the room. Once they stowed the plunger and tools away, they left through the front door of the lodge.

It felt good to be by Chase's side, to work together with him. Show him a little of who she was.

But the closeness also gave her pause. Lexi could no longer ignore what she knew to be true.

Her heart was in serious trouble.

Walking away from the lodge, Chase didn't know what to think about the woman next to him.

Lexi took everything in stride. She seemed to be all in. Surprising him the most was that she laughed. It was a gorgeous laugh. To top it off, he didn't know what to do with those amusing socks. He just knew everything that had happened today had done nothing but intrigue him.

And he wasn't sure how he felt about that.

Her hair was different. Long, shiny, with curls at the end. It looked soft. She looked soft tonight. Feminine. Intriguing.

There was that word again.

As they crossed the field, the sun gave his land the last bit of light. She shoved her hands in her pockets.

"Where's your coat?" he asked.

"I think I left it in your truck."

He stopped midstride and yanked off his canvas barn jacket and turned to her. Annoyed, he said, "You can't go anywhere on this property without a jacket. We might be having an abnormally warm spring, but you never know when the wind is going to pick up. This land will do a lot, but there aren't trees to block that wind when it shows up."

Her pink nose scrunched. She looked cute. And cold. "Are you upset with me?"

He held out the coat for her to slip her arms into, then turned her to him. It dwarfed her. She still looked cute. "I'm not upset," he said, pulling together the sides of the coat just under the collar. "I'm just—"

He locked his eyes with hers.

Intrigued. He was just intrigued. Heading straight toward enthralled, and he wasn't sure he wanted to go there right now.

But the next thing he knew, he was pulling her to him, slowly. Her eyes grew round, but she drew closer, placed her hands on his forearms.

He was about an inch away from kissing her. He squeezed his eyes closed and gritted his teeth. "I'm just concerned about you, Lexi," he whispered. "I don't want you to catch cold."

"Nothing's going to happen to me, Chase," she said softly.

But she couldn't guarantee that.

"Chase," a man called from behind him.

He immediately released Lexi, and she swayed, then stepped back.

Hunter was right. Chase was an idiot. What was he thinking?

Turning, he saw Nate and Harper Forrester dressed in jeans, sweatshirts and jackets walking toward them. Then he was hit with something else. After just being on the ranch for the day, the couple appeared more relaxed. Nate's military gait was almost unnoticeable, and he held his wife's hand. Harper's face looked fresh, as if a few hours on the land had given her a little bit of peace.

Chase stared at the couple. This was it. This was what he'd dreamed of giving to military personnel and their families. He wanted to take Lexi's hand in his and somehow tell her what this moment meant to him. But he didn't dare pull her close again.

Nate greeted him with a handshake.

"We got your bathroom back in full working order," Chase said. "I apologize for the inconvenience."

Lexi cleared her throat next to him and he glanced down at her. She'd pulled her lips in and to her credit was not saying a word. But her eyes danced.

"Sorry." Chase ran a hand through his hair. "Nate. Harper. This is Lexi Gardner, and she's actually the one who got your bathroom back to normal."

Harper looked to Lexi, and they both laughed.

Lexi shook their hands in greeting, aiming a megawatt smile at them, and said, "I'm so glad you're here."

"I am, too," Harper said. "We've been roaming around exploring the property today and there's something really special about this place."

"Thank you. Like I said this morning, you are our first official military guests. We hope to expand not just to more people staying at the lodge, but we have land farther out where we'd like to build individual cabins and add more recreation and emotional support options for families."

For a second, he wondered when he'd hear from the contractor. Then he worried if he'd have the money to start the project. Pressure began to build in his chest. But when he glanced at the Forresters, those details faded away. Four Cross Ranch was helping people, just like he'd dreamed it would.

Lexi beamed. She seemed to be truly proud of his place, and there was nothing to do with that but file it away with the other things he was learning and liked about her.

Harper looked between Chase and Lexi. "How do you two know each other?"

"Oh, um…" He looked over at Lexi.

She only came up with, "Well, uh…"

They stared at each other, and he realized they probably looked like two deer caught in the headlights.

The wind swirled around them. Why couldn't he say anything? Better—what was he supposed to say? Lexi bit her lip.

Then it hit him. He turned to the Forresters and said, "She's my fiancée." When he put his arm around her, she was stiffer than a new saddle.

Nothing surprised him more than the fact that those words didn't hurt him. Those words actually sounded natural.

Harper clapped her hands and squealed. "Oh, that's so wonderful. Congratulations!"

But Nate's brow furrowed. "You made your fiancée work on the toilet? I know we're the ones here to restore our marriage, but you might want to rethink some things as well."

The group's laughter filled the field, two cows in the next pasture over even chiming in with their cattle calls.

When the chuckles died down, Harper asked, "When is the wedding?"

Without missing a beat, Lexi said, "In three weeks."

Twenty-one days until her birthday, but who was counting.

Harper looked at her husband and smiled. "You know what I have to ask them, right?"

The man nodded sagely. "We learned the hard way. I think you should."

She turned to Lexi and asked, "Have you gotten your marriage license yet?"

Reality slammed into Chase's chest.

Looking as stunned as Chase felt, Lexi said, "Oh, um… no, not yet."

Harper stepped closer to Lexi and placed her hand on Lexi's arm. "You might want to get on that soon. We rushed our wedding because of a deployment and forgot that one tiny detail that actually makes you legally married."

"Oh," Lexi said. Chase had been married before but had completely forgotten. What if they'd made it to her birthday only to ruin the entire plan because they never went to the courthouse to get their marriage license?

"It all turned out okay." Harper turned her smiling face to her husband and softened her tone. "Everything all turned out okay in the end."

Chase stepped back. "Thank you for the advice," he said. "We'll take care of that this week." At his side, Lexi stood ramrod straight, but he kept talking. "For now, you two go on down to the lodge. Enjoy a fire in the fireplace. We have s'more ingredients laid out for you on the kitchen counter."

"We saw that earlier," Harper said. "Such a nice touch. You've gone to great lengths to make us feel so welcome. And I love the throw pillow in the master bedroom."

Throw pillow?

"The one about the spurs," she said, and then it hit him. Lexi's ridiculous three-dollar pillow. "It's super cute and hilarious."

A wide smile split across Lexi's face. It was almost as bright as the few stars that had come out to twinkle in the last few minutes.

After saying their farewells for the evening, Chase looked down at Lexi. "You're going to rub this in my face, aren't you."

She aimed her smile at him, and he decided he didn't care if she did. "I'm not going to rub it in your face," she said. "But I do think I'm going to ask for full dispensation over the throw pillows in our marriage and at the lodge."

He narrowed his eyes. "I'm going to regret this, aren't I."

Something serious crossed her face, then her features softened and she whispered, "I hope not."

He pulled in a long breath, then released it, never taking his eyes from her. He hoped she never had any regrets with him either.

"Chase?" she asked, vulnerability reflecting in her eyes.

"Right here, Lexi."

"Are we really going to get our marriage license this week?"

After a beat, he answered, "Yes."

Chapter Seven

Standing on the steps of the county courthouse, the idea of getting a marriage license fell with a thud to the bottom of Chase's stomach. No more musings about the intriguing sides of Lexi Gardner. No more thoughts of growing old together on the ranch with someone whose company he enjoyed. No more wondering if they could really make this bizarre situation work.

No. Standing on the steps of the courthouse with the morning Wyoming sun beating down on him only brought back flashes of Lexi's terrified face as Mildred bucked her. And the fear that saturated every cell in Chase as he tried to figure out how to save her.

He just didn't know if he could make a lifelong commitment to another woman. What if tragedy fell on Lexi the way it came to his wife?

He wiped his hands on his jeans. He'd worn his good pair for the occasion.

Lexi stepped closer and lowered her voice. "You okay?"

He glanced at her and found her eyes held the same anxiety he felt. "Yeah. You?"

"I'm fine," she said, her entire body stilted. Delicate stitched flowers lined the sleeves and neck of her flowing white shirt. Her jean skirt hit her at the knees. And what he now deemed as her fancy boots completed the ensemble.

She wore her hair down today in soft curls. He didn't know if she did any of this for him, but she sure looked beautiful.

Stilted. And beautiful.

They stood side by side and stared at the tall glass doors of the courthouse.

"Are we both lying?" he asked without looking at her.

"Yes," she said.

Slowly, they turned their heads to each other and locked eyes. It only took two point five seconds for them to burst out laughing.

"I'm sorry." She giggled through the words and placed her hand on his arm. "I'm so nervous."

"I know." He chuckled. "I don't know why I thought this would be no big deal."

"Well…" She cleared her throat. "It isn't that big of a deal if we think of it logically. It's like you said. I have seventeen days until my birthday. If we get the marriage license now, it takes the pressure off both of us. We don't sign it until we're sure we want to get married. And—" her voice gentled "—if we decide that it isn't best to get married, we throw it away. No harm done."

"No harm done," he repeated, the depth of her brown eyes drawing him in.

But for some reason, Chase felt like there would be harm done. To which one of them, he didn't quite know.

What he did know was that over the last week, he had come to care for Lexi. Which is why he proposed they get their marriage license today. At the time, it had felt like a solid decision. Logical. Safe.

Staring at the doors of the courthouse, Chase felt anything but safe.

When the proposition to marry Lexi first came up, he was intent on her marrying someone because they treasured her. His problem now was that the more time they spent to-gether, the more he found *himself* treasuring her. His feel-ings bounced between total enjoyment at being with her and the debilitating fear of ever losing her.

But worse. He couldn't reconcile considering marriage with the trust money that came with her. The closer they got to her birthday, the more he understood only a fraction of the stress Lexi had endured over this money.

He stood by their decision to get the marriage license today. Though a small gesture, it did put a dent in the pres-sure that continued to build to her birthday.

He took his Stetson off and placed it over his heart. "If we get married, Lexi, I promise you, it will be a sincere partnership. True friendship. I would honor you in every way that I could."

"I know, Chase," she said with quiet confidence. "It's who you are. It's why I picked you. Why I trust you."

Her trust in him almost leveled him every day. What she couldn't understand was that while she carried the burden of the trust, he carried the burden of being chosen by her. It was not something he'd ever share with her. She didn't need more weight to carry on her shoulders.

"All right," he said in all seriousness, "I just need to know one thing before we head inside."

She straightened her spine and took a deep breath. "Okay."

He narrowed his eyes, purposefully adding drama to the moment. "What do your socks say today?"

Lowering her chin just a touch, she looked up at him through her lashes and gave him a coy smile. "I'm not tell-ing."

"What?" He feigned hurt. "We are about to get a document that could tie us together for the rest of our lives, and you can't tell me what your socks say? Today, of all days?"

Lexi laughed and shook her head. "I'll tell you on the way out of the courthouse."

He sighed a fake-exasperated sigh, truly glad that they were laughing together. With their decision feeling less burdensome, he held out his hand for her. When she put her palm in his, he led her up the stairs and to the county clerk's office.

To get a marriage license.

Because maybe they were getting married.

Or maybe they weren't.

Holding a manila envelope with an unsigned marriage license in his hand, and a whole bunch of questions in his heart, Chase walked to his truck with Lexi at his side. His phone buzzed from his back pocket. When he saw what was on the screen, he slowed his strides.

"Chase? Everything okay?" Lexi asked.

Looking up from his phone, he said, "It's Nate Forrester."

She cocked her head. "Why do you have a strange look on your face?"

He took off his hat and ran a hand through his hair. "This has been a good week for the Forresters. So good that they want to renew their vows and wondered if it was possible to do that while they're here."

Her face lit up and she grabbed his arm. Excitement rolled off her, and she bounced on her toes. "That's great news. This is exactly what you hoped the nonprofit could offer people. Rest, restoration, maybe a new beginning."

The contradictory weight of the text crashed down on him. It was such good news, but at the same time a big ask.

"Lexi. They leave tomorrow. How am I going to pull this off for this evening knowing I'm needed at the ranch?" He'd checked the records last night and they still had a substantial number of heifers waiting to calve.

She mimed like she was rolling up her sleeves and shot a confident smile his way. "Then I've got my work cut out for me."

"You don't get it. It's too much. You're under deadline, too. I'm sure you have work today."

"You're the one that doesn't get it. It's too much for one person. But it's not too much for *us*." She nudged his side with her elbow. "Besides, I'll work after the reception. This won't be the first all-nighter I've pulled during tax season."

His entire body blanched. "Reception? I didn't even think of that. Do they need a reception, too?"

She threw her head back and laughed. "Chase, what were you going to do? Renew their vows on the porch tomorrow morning while they're packing their car?" She tugged on his arm. "This is special. And I know how to help pull this off."

They locked eyes, and he couldn't seem to stop staring. She held him captivated.

Gently, she leaned her weight into his side and asked, "Do you trust me?"

He'd never felt like he and Lexi made a good team before. But right now, with her pressed against him, hope filling her eyes, he'd sign over his best bull to her if she asked.

"All right." He put his arm through hers. "Lead the way."

Eight hours later, Chase found himself outside of the chow hall wrestling a necktie. He'd rather be out wrestling a cow, but he felt drawn to the Forresters' vow renewal. The more he thought about it today, the more he dreamed of plans for Four Cross Hope. What else could God do on his land for military families?

Standing next to him, Lexi asked, "Can I put you out of your misery and help you with that?"

"I basically left everything else to you today. You'd think the least I could do was dress myself."

She stepped toward him, and he offered her the mangled black fabric that hung around his neck. "It wasn't hard," she said. "Harper found a dress in town, and the pastor was available. The ranch cook easily made tonight's barbecue dinner for a slightly larger crowd. I just put a few things together for the reception. Today actually gave me some great ideas for the nonprofit."

"Does that mean we're going to be arguing about purchasing budgets soon?"

"Well—" she glanced from the tie to him "—we're due a good disagreement. This week has thrown me off."

He couldn't agree more.

The abysmal knot he'd created with the fabric gave her a hard time. The same way her delicate wildflower perfume wreaked havoc with his senses. Why did her hair seem glossier tonight? And why did he notice that her hair seemed glossier? Probably because of the Kelly green sweaterdress she was wearing.

Her first attempt at the tie failed.

He lowered his chin to look at her, bringing their faces dangerously close. "I don't think you're doing much better with my tie than I was," he murmured.

She blinked and shook her head. "Anything's better than the noose you created," she said, getting back on task.

Good. He should get back on task, too. He couldn't be thinking this way about her.

When she finished with the tie, she patted him twice on the

chest. "When you walk in, you'll see that we split the room into two halves. The ceremony on the left with the awning and chairs, and the reception on the right with the tables. The Forresters asked us to sit in the front row, either side, for the ceremony."

He studied her face. "You look pretty tonight, Lexi," he said softly.

Okay. Apparently, he *was* going to think this way about her.

A light blush hit her cheeks. "You clean up real well yourself, cowboy."

He nodded, having no clue what to say. He might have put on a nice shirt and tie with his jeans and boots for the vow renewal, but he certainly didn't hold a candle to her glow tonight.

When he entered the chow hall, he couldn't believe the transformation. The room was usually completely utilitarian, full of unadorned tables and chairs to feed the staff on the ranch. Tonight, it was transformed with fabric-covered chairs, tablecloths, tiny candles, and flower arrangements. He'd have to ask Lexi where she got all of this stuff.

A few minutes later, with the Forresters' best friends who'd driven three hours from Denver, the ranch staff, the Stimpsons, a few families from town, Hunter, and Chase and Lexi looking on, pastor Beckett Gentry officiated Nate and Harper Forrester's recommitment to each other.

Chase never considered himself a fan of weddings. But this moment felt a little bit sweet and a whole lot significant. He knew the pressure that came with keeping a military marriage together. By the grace of God, his marriage with Laura took hold. And by the grace of God, Nate and Harper seemed stronger than ever.

Which gave Chase an odd thought. Would God grant

someone even more grace to hold a second marriage together?

But this kind of thinking would only lead him somewhere he didn't want to return to in his lifetime. Loving another woman.

Losing one spouse was enough. Lexi might not be the quiet adventurer that his wife was, but that didn't mean marriage to Lexi would come without risk. God only knew the number of days anyone had. He'd learned that the hard way. In the most ironic turn of events, instead of Chase losing his life while serving his country on deployment, his wife had died right here on a Wyoming mountain.

No. He might be getting married a second time, but he wouldn't be trusting God with his love for another woman again.

Once on the floor of the chow hall, all thoughts of Lexi went out the window. It was strictly survival mode. Helping with food service on the buffet line and keeping up with small talk was about all he could muster after the day he'd had in the pastures.

Lexi, on the other hand, worked the room as if she was the perfect hostess, gliding between tables and gifting people with easy laughter.

Chase cringed inwardly as he tried to charm the guests. He was never good with people. He was dependable. Consistent. He was the man to get the job done. But he was not a people person.

He glanced at Lexi, who effortlessly served their guests with a genuine smile and interest in their short conversations.

Something hit him in the chest.

She balanced him. Her strengths filled the gaps of his

weaknesses. He rubbed the spot over his heart, but the tightness wouldn't go away.

Commotion from the kitchen broke him out of his thoughts.

Three people flanked a three-tier cake as they walked through the swinging kitchen door. Its simplicity gave it beauty. Cream-colored icing with delicate polka dots covered the layers, and a row of beaded icing that looked like a pearl necklace circled the base of each tier. Four tall, skinny gold candles stood at the top, their flames sparking and illuminating the servers' smiles as they carefully walked toward the Forresters' table.

How in the world Lexi pulled that cake off, he could not imagine.

Adrianna, the kitchen hand farthest from him, announced, "Four Cross Ranch would like to give a warm congratulations to Mr. and Mrs. Forrester on their happy occasion."

Everyone clapped their well-wishes. A few offered cheers and whistles.

Chase scanned the room and found Lexi a few feet from the couple. When he caught her gaze, he grinned. She nodded in kind, a sweet smile on her lips.

But she broke their connection, glanced in front of her, and a look of horror morphed across her face.

When Chase followed her line of sight, he watched helplessly as one of the servers carrying the cake caught her hip on the edge of a chair and thrust the cake off-balance. Almost as if in slow motion, the top layer slid, its weight dragging the rest of the cake off the plate like a tugboat.

Right into Nate Forrester's lap.

Collectively, everyone froze. Gasps popped throughout the room. Harper covered her mouth with both of her hands. Lexi stood stock-still, the color draining from her face.

But Chase took charge.

He approached the three cake servers, the one who got caught on the chair on the verge of tears. In a calm voice, he said, "Why don't the three of you head to the kitchen and grab supplies to help clean this up."

They nodded in unison and scurried away.

"Nate." Chase turned to the wife. "Harper. I'm sincerely sorry."

Slowly, Harper's hands drew down from her mouth and revealed a huge smile. She burst out laughing. "I'm not," she said, waving her hand in front of her face, her words almost unintelligible because of her cackling. "That was one of the funniest things I've ever seen."

A few guests allowed their shoulders to shake and looked sheepishly around at each other. Several others started chuckling.

Contagious, the humor spread through the room in waves of murmurs and laughter.

The pit in Chase's stomach loosened a little.

Nate appeared put-out. He tilted his head to the side and looked at his wife, shaking his head. "I'm so glad this is entertaining you."

"I've got to get a picture of you like this to send to your platoon," his wife replied. She cracked herself up with her own comment and laughed harder.

Barely noticeable, Nate's lips tipped at the end while he continued to shake his head.

Lexi's panicked gaze darted from person to person across the room.

One of the servers brought white utilitarian kitchen towels and a small trash can. "One of the towels is dry, and one is wet with water in case that helps," she murmured.

Lexi may kill him for what he was about to do, but Chase thought it was the right thing under the circumstances.

"Nate, again, I apologize. I'd like to help in any way I can. We'll arrange and pay for dry cleaning."

"That's not necessary," Nate said with a resigned shrug and good-natured smile. "It's just a little sugar, flour and eggs."

Chase couldn't read Lexi's face. But she snapped to the situation and stepped forward. "Harper, I'll have a special dessert delivery brought to the ranch as soon as possible. Could we invite everyone to the dance floor while we wait?"

Two guests murmured jokes of spilling your cake and eating it too while they headed for the open dance space. Nate and Harper excused themselves to get Nate cleaned up and into a new set of clothes while Chase pitched in to change the linens of the table and switch out Nate's chair.

Lexi excused herself and made a call.

Chase didn't know what she had up her sleeve.

He went to the kitchen to clean up, mingled with a few guests, then headed to the buffet tables and put two plates of food together for Lexi and himself. She had to be as starving as he was by now.

Twenty minutes later, Lexi backed into the swinging kitchen door with a giant smile of pride and satisfaction on her face. "One gorgeous German chocolate cake has just been delivered to the chow hall and is being cut as I stand here and breathe."

He shook his head at her. "You're going to have to explain how that happened, but first—" he nodded to the plates in his hands "—I'm headed out to the back deck. Come with me and we'll finally eat."

The large wooden porch held six sturdy metal chairs where they sat down to enjoy their food.

After Chase handed Lexi a plate, napkin and utensils, they ate in companionable silence.

Music floated through mounted speakers. A country singer crooned about love, and Chase looked at Lexi.

He wiped his fingers and his mouth with his napkin, stood and offered her a hand. "Dance with me."

Her mouth parted, soft surprise in her eyes.

"Come on," he said. "Fertilizer, plumbing repairs, un-expected event planning and cake disasters are a lot to ask of one woman over the course of a week. But maybe I can make it up to you with a dance."

The corner of her mouth lifted, and she nodded.

He held out his left hand for her to place hers and wrapped his other arm around her waist. She fit perfectly, and he didn't know how he felt about that. He had held an-other woman once who fit perfectly.

"Thank you for dinner," she said. "It was right up my alley with Gardner Economics because it was free."

Her tone told him she was trying to make a joke, but he stopped their movement and looked directly into her eyes. "Lexi. You're worth paying full price."

Surprise crossed her face, and she looked to the ground.

He didn't mean to make her uncomfortable. He didn't exactly know why he said what he did, except it continued to bother him that she seemed to consistently settle for less than she deserved.

"How in the world did you pull off that chocolate cake?" he asked as he shifted his feet for them to continue swaying.

"The baker in town, Alison Velasquez, is a client who lets me sample her yummy desserts. Lately, she's been test-ing her cakes. I knew she had two extras as of yesterday and called her. The first one was the disaster cake. The sec-ond one was the German chocolate cake. When she heard about the cause, she gave us a steep discount and free delivery herself."

His lips twitched. "And what is this in exchange for, oh President of the Gardner Economics Club?"

"Nothing, really. I found a tax exemption that saved her a lot of money this year. She said she was grateful."

He shook his head and locked gazes with her. "You're one of a kind, Lexi Gardner."

"Me? You're the one who dealt with the cake disaster. I was in such a panic." She released her hold on his hand and clutched her chest. "You kept your head and dealt with the entire situation."

"I thought you'd be mad at me for offering free dry cleaning."

"Sometimes spending is about calculating the degree of need." She swallowed and set her hand back in his. "But it can also be about doing the right thing. You were good in that crisis, Chase. I froze, but you were the real hero."

"I don't see it that way. You've spent the entire day and night adjusting and helping the Forresters at every turn."

She shrugged. "It was all hands on deck."

He squeezed her waist and deadpanned. "I'm an army man, ma'am."

"Sorry," she said on a giggle. "Whatever the case, your nonprofit is about to really come alive, Chase. This week went so well with the Forresters."

He drew back from her and studied her face. "You really believe in what I'm doing here, don't you."

"I do," she said without hesitation. Without qualifiers. Without scolding him about the budget issues. Her answer was honest at its core.

Somewhere in the evening, he'd gotten lost.

He thought he knew what tonight was going to be about.

They'd host a small ceremony and reception and call it a night.

Instead, he saw Lexi's work ethic, quick humor and her unexpected beauty.

He and Lexi worked well together. As if they were a team. As if tonight was orchestrated for them to navigate.

Together. He and Lexi.

Lexi needed to guide them out of this moment because she felt a pull toward Chase that had nothing to do with an innocent dance or a marriage of convenience. She guided them back inside.

"I mentioned earlier that I have some ideas for the ranch."

He blinked, his brow drawing down. "Yes?"

"Well. When we visited Bright Horizons, Mrs. Harding told me she married off the last of her four daughters and didn't know what to do with the centerpieces because she didn't need them anymore. So I had already made arrangements to pick up those supplies before this vow renewal had even come up."

Chase looked down at her and cocked an eyebrow.

"They're perfect." Lexi walked over to one of the empty tables and pulled the clear, round vase toward them. "We can save all of these items for future events. The vases are classic. The smooth river rocks are a wonderful tie-in to the land around us. We fill the vases with the rocks and then use foliage, flowers, flags, beads, ribbons or whatever someone comes up with to decorate however we want. You can use anything, really, depending on the event theme. And it's all free."

"Where are you going with this?"

"Chase—" she put her hand on his arm "—the Forresters won't be the only couple who wants to renew their vows to each other. My understanding is that the chow hall isn't in use all the time. We could use it as a multipurpose area."

Understanding dawned on him, and his face took on a look of wonder.

"Or maybe we have birthday parties or holiday celebrations. Festivals and carnivals. We'll get a storage closet and keep all of this stuff." She held her hand out to the chow hall. "And then I can bargain shop for more decor along the way. Maybe trade with local artisans for their work to use at events. The possibilities are endless, really. The event closet can grow with the nonprofit."

"You've outdone yourself," Chase said in a tone that made Lexi feel both giddy and proud.

But then she thought of her recent financial decision for the ranch that wasn't free, and tension tightened in her shoulders. Especially since she had yet to tell Chase. She tried to rub the pain out of the muscle.

"Hey," Chase said, concern lining his eyes. "You okay?"

"Well, I suppose I should just come clean." She huffed out a long breath. "I called the builder. The one you targeted to contract for the new cabins for the veterans."

Chase crossed his arms and nodded.

"Originally, we had him slated to start early next year, and I was checking to see when he needed the deposit. But he shared that he recently bought out his competitor, which means he has more manpower, which means—"

"He can start sooner."

"Yes."

Chase rubbed his chin, now slightly darkened with a five-o'clock shadow. "But we don't have the funds."

"Not exactly. We can come up with the deposit for him to start."

"But…"

"But paying him is contingent upon other things." Things like a solid yield from their crops of hay. Avoiding unexpected repairs on ranch property. And maybe a marriage that would open a trust fund.

He stayed completely still but narrowed his eyes. "What did you tell him?"

As if someone turned a crank on a machine, the muscles in her shoulders tightened one notch higher. Her dry mouth wouldn't let her say anything. There were two parts of her at war. The accountant in her yelled warnings, and her heart yelled back a reply to take her worries elsewhere.

"Lexi. What did you tell him?"

She slid her eyes to the side. "I told him to come on Monday to get the lay of the land and that I'd set up a meeting with you."

Three long beats later, Chase threw his head back and laughed.

"What's so funny?"

He leveled his eyes on her. "Since my accountant made a risky choice, is this a good time to tell my accountant that *I* did something *she* won't approve of?"

"Have at it."

"I booked rooms at the lodge for next week. A veteran's family of four. Everyone in need of rest and recuperation." He cringed almost apologetically. "They arrive in two days."

"We can get the rooms ready in two days." But that meant that he was going to pay their expenses so they wouldn't have to worry about the cost of their room, board and recreation. Lexi pictured numbers on an antique cash register spinning higher and higher.

If the ranch was not only going to absorb the cost, but not profit from those accommodations, this was a problem. Especially after booking the builder.

Once again, her heart yelled louder than the accountant in her. Chase was talking about real people, in need, without resources.

They would simply have to find another way to get additional funding.

Stress that felt like an ice pick now stabbed her shoulders.

Or.

Chase and Lexi would really get married, and these mounting financial obligations wouldn't be a problem.

Chase ran a hand over his face, uncertainty behind his eyes that now looked tired. She couldn't be sure, but he must be having similar thoughts to hers.

Carrying a piece of wedding cake, Hunter sauntered toward them. "Congratulations to the bride and groom," he said.

Her entire body locked tight, and Chase seemed to freeze in place. Chase told her he hadn't shared with anyone that they went to get their marriage license today. Neither had she.

Hunter's eyes darted between the two of them. "I meant the Forresters, seeing as how I'm eating a piece of their wedding cake. But is there something you two need to share?"

Chase cleared his throat and shifted his stance, a picture of discomfort. "No. Nothing. Nothing to share."

Without saying a word, Hunter shoveled cake into his mouth. His piercing eyes held Lexi's. Once he swallowed, he asked, "How are you feeling, Lexi? Any pain or soreness still lingering after the incident with Mildred and the snake?"

Hunter's question turned his brother into a statue. Chase's

eyes glazed over with a hint of fear, and it looked like his breathing had shallowed.

"I'm fine. That seems forever ago," she said to Hunter, though she stared at Chase. "Perfectly fine."

"That's good to hear." Hunter sent a keen look at his brother, then crammed the other half of the piece of cake into his mouth. With a nod to both of them, he walked away.

Not for the first time, Lexi wondered what kind of woman would catch Hunter's heart.

When she turned to Chase, he was in the same pose.

"Chase." Lexi placed a hand on his arm and quieted her voice. "I really am fine. You know that. It happened days ago." She squeezed.

He looked down at her, something fierce warring behind his eyes. "I do," he said, his voice gruff. "But it could have been different."

It could have. It could have been different, like his wife.

She knew. Oh, how she knew. The day after the snake incident, she sat alone in the Four Cross lodge and stared at the picture of Laura. Lexi didn't know why she did it. Maybe she was looking for the woman in the picture to talk back to her. To tell her how to get Chase past his fear.

But that wasn't logical. If her reputation was accurate, Laura was fearless, not reckless. But not afraid to take risks others would not. She was the reason for all of his fears.

Lexi looked at Chase and said the most distracting thing she could think of to pull him out of his dark place. "I completely forgot to tell you what my socks say today."

One slow blink, then a spark in his eyes. "You're right. What do your socks say today?"

Her face heated, and she just knew she was blushing. She leaned her weight into his arm and whispered, "My socks are white with pink letters that say 'Bride.'"

His entire body jerked. He blinked again, this time as if he were perplexed. Or confused. Maybe angry? "Bride?"

She placed her hand on her collarbone and stepped back, mortification spreading through her. "I'm sorry. I thought—" she shook her head "—I thought it would be funny. Because we got the papers today for the marriage license. I mean, we aren't married until we sign them, but technically I'm the…" her voice trailed off along with her confidence "…bride."

"Sure." He paused, sounding unsure, then nodded. "Sure. Absolutely. Bride."

Now both her heart and her inner accountant were yelling at her. Along with her brain and ego. She'd made a misstep in sharing that information with him, especially after Hunter's question had reminded Chase of the horse incident. She had to redirect. Now.

"Um, why don't we go say hello to the Stimpsons?" she asked.

"Sure," he mumbled. "I have to talk to the foreman first. Go on without me, and I'll join you in a minute."

Before Lexi could answer, Chase bolted across the room. Her emotions deflated.

Chase had darted from her faster than one of his horses. Why did it feel like her groom was running away?

And why did she feel like she got married today without actually getting married?

They'd gone to the courthouse for a marriage license only to come back to the ranch for someone else's wedding and reception. Everything felt a little real.

Lexi knew she picked her favorite white shirt to go to the courthouse because it made her feel pretty.

Also, because it was white.

Chase showing up with a clean shave, pressed jeans and a blue shirt that set off his eyes didn't help.

But tonight, he looked even more handsome.

As she watched Chase across the room, she prayed he would forget about her socks. Forget about Hunter's ill-timed reminder. Forget about the pain his wife's death caused him.

Because she had a problem.

If we get married, Lexi, I promise you, it would be a sincere partnership. True friendship. I would honor you in every way that I could.

What if she no longer wanted a nice partnership with Chase?

What if she wanted something real with the cowboy veteran?

He couldn't give that to her.

Not only that, she was starting to wonder if she shouldn't ask him to give her a platonic marriage.

She cared for him. She cared for him in a way that she didn't know if she should ask him to do something he said he would never do again.

Yes, she had a problem.

The only way to move forward was to do the one thing she promised him she would do, which was to help the non-profit. She would spend the next two days getting ready for their new guests and hope her feelings leveled out.

Chapter Eight

Chase stood on the far side of his property with the weight of his body leaned into his forearms atop the brown wooden fence.

It didn't matter that he'd checked in a family of four earlier this week. Or that, even if the bid for building the cabins took his breath away, his time talking with the contractor gave him new vigor for the nonprofit. Today was different. Today, clouds dimmed the morning with a shadow of sorrow.

The smell of grass, manure and a hint of something that could only be described as Wyoming sat with him.

His hat hung low on his face. Maybe it'd hide the tears that streamed down his cheeks.

Once a year.

Once a year, he allowed himself to cry over his wife's death.

With his eyes locked on the Snowy Range, he shook his head. Every day, Medicine Bow Peak dared to show its face to him. It seemed especially cruel today. It had taken Laura from him.

He'd never understood her sense of adventure. It seemed out of control. Unnecessary. The military had forced him to live a life full of risk. But he never took risks for fun.

Laura thrived on danger.

She'd been younger than him by eight years and chasing a dream to ski in the Olympics. They'd put off having kids for that reason. When he'd left for his last deployment, they both knew she'd never compete at the top level. They both knew he'd come home, and they'd finally start a family.

But the mountain took her.

Something Chase couldn't fathom God allowing. The Almighty could move mountains. But He couldn't move this one? He couldn't simply allow them to start their family?

Chase groaned something guttural. He knew God was trustworthy. Sometimes he just didn't understand exactly what he was trusting.

"At least you died doing something you loved, Laura," his raspy voice whispered to the mountain.

An eagle soared into his vision, but Chase didn't break his line of sight from the snowy peak.

He heard the heavy crunch of grass behind him. Knew who it would be without looking. Using his coat sleeve, he wiped away any remnants of his grief.

The smell of strong coffee hit him before his brother edged into view. Hunter handed him a cup and kept a second mug for himself.

The brothers stood in an identical pose, weight forward into the fence, cups between their hands. Steam rose from their drinks and disappeared into the air.

"Five years," Hunter said.

Chase grunted.

"That mountain move yet?"

"Excuse me?" Chase asked, not breaking his focus.

"You've been standing out here awhile in the same position. I figure you're waiting for that mountain to move."

"Maybe I am." He lifted the hot coffee and took a swig, ignoring the burn as it went down. "Maybe I am."

Without warning, Hunter said, "Your mother-in-law is here."

The coffee Chase just drank got stuck in his throat. He coughed, the hot liquid punishing him while he tried to swallow it down.

Hunter pounded Chase's back but remained facing forward.

When Chase's throat had mostly recovered, he clarified. "Laura's mother is here?"

"I left her at the lodge with some coffee. Told her I'd come get you."

When Chase was married, he wasn't in country long enough to be close with his mother-in-law. But on the occasions they were together, they had a playful banter he enjoyed. A mutual respect because of the woman in common who they loved.

He had no clue why she would show up unannounced.

"She have a reason?" he asked.

"No."

Even though he knew he should move, the mountain held his gaze. Somewhere deep inside, Chase wanted something from this mountain. Normally, he figured he just wanted answers from God. But this year was different. He just didn't understand what about it was different.

Hunter looked down at his boots and scuffed a toe once on the ground. "I can cover for you if you want."

"No." Chase scrubbed a hand down his face and pulled off the fence. "I'll go."

But as he turned, something churned in his gut. He glanced back to the spot where he imagined he lost his wife.

What do you want from me? he internally asked the mountain. Maybe he was asking his wife. Maybe God.

Hunter walked to the lodge by Chase's side in silence. When they arrived, he asked, "Want me to go with you?"

Chase gave Hunter a hearty pat on the shoulder. "No. Thanks, though."

When Chase walked into the dining room, he spotted Barbara. Petite, strawberry blond hair and a pert nose, she looked just like her daughter. The years had been kind to Barbara, though he'd always thought Laura's death robbed her of her vitality. Impeccably dressed, as always, in slacks and a silk shirt, she sipped from a coffee mug, her head held high. But from where he stood, Chase could see the dark circles under her eyes.

When she spotted him, a smile broke over her face although the familiar sparkle in her eyes seemed dimmer. Laura used to have that same sparkle.

His boots felt cemented to the ground, but he forced himself to pick his feet up and move toward her.

She rose to greet him.

But after a few heavy steps, he heard his name called behind him. When he turned, he froze.

"Hi there."

His entire body locked tight.

Lexi.

Lexi, who wore her hair down today and smelled like wildflowers. Lexi, who had asked him to marry her.

Lexi, who didn't know Chase was meeting his mother-in-law.

She smiled expectantly at him.

Chase wanted to hop on a train with a one-way ticket out of Wyoming. He cleared his throat. *Keep it simple. Profes-*

sional. "Hi, Lexi. What brings you to Four Cross Ranch today?"

At his side, he felt Barbara's presence, but he didn't dare look at her. Maybe he could move Lexi along quickly.

Lexi glanced at Barbara, then back to him. From her large purse, she pulled out something wrapped in a grocery bag. "You mentioned that the family staying here needed diaper wipes."

Barbara held her hand out to Lexi. "I'm Barbara Hartwell."

Returning the greeting, Lexi introduced herself. "What brings you to the ranch today, Ms. Hartwell?"

"I'm Chase's mother-in-law," she said proudly. But her next words were more subdued. "Today is the fifth anniversary of my daughter's death. Chase's wife."

The color drained out of Lexi's face. "I'm so very sorry for your loss." She shook her head as if she was trying to shake away the pain of the moment. "I'm sorry to say that I never met Laura. But I've heard many wonderful things about her."

"She was a quiet soul, but a force to be reckoned with." Barbara looped her arm around Chase's and leaned in. "I was thrilled when she married Chase. He was the perfect match for her, and she was the perfect match for him."

Lexi's pallor turned ashen.

"I don't remember a time when you two argued." His mother-in-law looked up at him, her watery gaze reaching back five years. "You two were made for each other. That kind of match only comes once in a lifetime."

Chase didn't miss how Lexi took a step back, holding the grocery package to her chest as if it were a shield.

"How do you two know each other?" Barbara asked him.

The question zinged around the room on a boomerang of anxiety.

Lexi works for me. She pushes all my buttons. She asked me to marry her. She's the first person who forces me to consider that there might be more for me in this life. Chase stood frozen in the tension of Barbara's question and didn't like it one bit.

Lexi's eyes darted between Chase and Barbara. She cleared her throat, but her voice still croaked. "I'm an accountant and do some work for the ranch." She took another step back and started talking faster. "I can see you're busy, Chase. I'll just leave these here on the counter." Another step backward, this time she caught her hip on the edge of the island. When she righted, she said, "It was so nice to meet you, Ms. Hartwell. Again, I'm sorry for your loss."

Before Chase could figure out how to smooth over the situation, Lexi was gone, and Barbara stared up at him with questions in her eyes.

The problem was, Chase probably had the same questions. But he didn't have a clue how to answer them.

Lexi tore through the lodge hallway praying that the tears would stay at bay.

That kind of match only comes once in a lifetime.

She hightailed it to her car.

That kind of match only comes once in a lifetime.

After turning the key to her ignition with more force than necessary, she hauled off the ranch property without looking back.

On the country roads, her hands shook. Her breath came unevenly. And her nose stung.

Soon her vision would blur, and it wouldn't be safe to drive.

She pulled over to a scenic overpass designated for sightseers. After parking, she looked across the rolling hills of prairie, all leading to the foothills of a mountain.

Staring at the mountain, tears began to leak out of her eyes.

"How could I have been so stupid?" she whispered to the white peak.

With no one to tell her she was wrong, she continued to heap judgment on herself. "He loved his wife. Of course he would never marry again. He and Laura never argued. They were perfect for each other. He still holds on to her through his mother-in-law."

Her face heated and the tears came faster. "He didn't dispute anything she said."

That kind of match only comes once in a lifetime.

It never came in Lexi's lifetime.

A sob rose in her throat, and she felt like it was choking her.

She could not take her eyes off the mountain. "Lord. How could I have gotten everything so wrong? How could I have picked so poorly? Three times now."

But she didn't think she picked poorly with Chase. His heart was just with another. How could she ask him to marry again when he didn't want that for himself?

A question rose from the depth of her soul. One she'd known was there, but one that she didn't have the courage to ask. With her heartache releasing into the quiet space of her car, she whispered, "Lord, what do You think of me?"

The tears finally slowed, and she drew in a deep breath. Popping open the glove compartment, she found a small packet of tissues. While she was drying her eyes, her phone buzzed in her pocket with a notification. When she pulled it out, the text message from her lawyer ricocheted her emotions and added another ingredient to the dread pooling in her stomach.

I'll be in town tomorrow. Do you have time to meet?

She didn't want to think about what her lawyer might have to say to her. Why did he want to meet her in person? To soften the blow that she couldn't get out of the conditions of the will? Or maybe he'd found a solution, and she had to sign some papers to get Chase and herself out of this situation?

Nothing felt right.

She took one more look at the mountain, drew in a long breath and texted back, What time?

The warm spring sun beat down on Chase's back as he pulled his clippers out of his back pocket.

Fence repair. He hated fence repair.

It gave him too much time to think. And today, he had way too many things fighting for attention in his brain.

At least his mostly loyal dog Duke was with him. Though he currently had no idea the exact whereabouts of the golden retriever.

The unexpected appearance of his former mother-in-law felt like he'd been thrown from a horse. Maybe experienced an unexpected infiltration on the battlefield. He hadn't talked to Lexi since yesterday. Her reply to his phone call had been a short text about work.

His worlds had collided, and he hadn't the faintest clue how to handle things.

Barbara Hartwell's perspective on his relationship with Laura was muddied in grief.

The temptation to make the deceased perfect in memory could be strong. Chase felt it with Laura. It was easier to remember the good. But Barbara's memory had thrown a veil of inaccuracy over her imperfect daughter. And her imperfect son-in-law. It hadn't been an appropriate time to say anything. Laura's mother was deeply grieving the five-year loss of her only daughter.

But the look on Lexi's face when she realized who Barbara was to Chase about did him in. He'd watched her shut down right in front of him.

He should want that, right? Even if he married her—when he married her—in eleven days, he couldn't risk having feelings for Lexi. Or her having feelings for him. Barbara served as a reminder of what happened when he loved someone.

Devastating loss.

But when his phone rang, he still hoped it was Lexi.

What he would say to her, he had no clue. All he knew was that he wanted to know if she was okay and what message her socks said today.

The phone lit up instead with Hunter's name, and before he answered, he looked up at their family's land. He wasn't in the mood to talk to his brother.

He stabbed the screen to take the call and asked gruffly, "What do you want?"

"Still in that chipper mood I left you in this morning?"

"You banished me to fence repair."

"Mucking the stalls didn't seem to take the fire out of you last time. I had to up my game." After a pause, he added, "Clearly I'm going to have to come up with something else."

Chase rubbed his cheek with the back of his hand. "Is there something you need?"

"I had a question about Lexi."

Duke appeared out of nowhere, shaking his excited body

and rubbing up against Chase as if he knew Hunter had just mentioned Lexi's name.

He leaned down and rubbed his dog's back. "What about Lexi?"

"I was just thinking." A prop plane flew overhead, and Chase followed it across the sky while his brother talked. "If you don't care about her, which you claim you don't, then what's the big deal in marrying her? What difference does it make?"

"Hunter—"

"But if you do care about her, which after what I saw at the reception it seems that you might, then why wouldn't you just marry her now?"

Chase shook his head, already tired of the short phone call. Why was his brother bringing this up now? "Hunter—"

"Either way, you care about her or you don't, it feels like you should think about it."

Duke jumped up and tried to lick Chase in the face. Chase wondered if this was a planned stealth attack by both his brother and his dog.

He released a labored sigh into the phone. "You know how I feel about getting married again."

"Good. Then you won't care that her lawyer's in town talking to her at the diner."

Chase's truck barreled down the highway. A bunch of wildflowers bound up with a red bandanna sat by his side, his Stetson firmly on his head.

It just felt like a time when a man needed his hat.

Duke hung his head out the passenger window, a look of determination on his golden retriever face that matched the storm stirring inside of Chase.

He had no clue why he brought his dog. Maybe as a last

resort. If he found out Lexi had done something ridiculous, he'd throw Duke at her to give her his puppy-dog eyes.

He wiped a hand over his face.

What a dumb plan.

All Chase knew was that his stomach clamped something fierce at the news that Lexi was at the diner with her lawyer. What if she'd changed her mind? What if, after seeing Chase with his former mother-in-law, she'd decided to do something rash? Her lawyer could misguide her. She could go back to her ex or find a mail-order groom.

The second Chase hit the diner, threw open the door and caught sight of Lexi across the room, he understood something else.

The thought of any man—who wasn't him—with her, no matter who it was, bothered him greatly.

When did that happen?

Lexi's eyes locked with his, her beautiful browns full of surprise. His chest rose and fell with his breathing, and he stared at her for a moment.

Yes. The thought of any man with Lexi, no matter who it was, bothered him greatly.

He saw his brother and Sheila out of the corner of his eye but ignored them and beelined it for Lexi.

Once he arrived at her table, he still only had eyes for her.

"Hey," she breathed, a slight blush hitting her cheeks.

The man across the booth from her, the lawyer he presumed, shifted and cleared his throat.

But Chase didn't take his eyes off Lexi. "Hey," he said.

He set the flowers on the table next to her, and her mouth gaped.

Placing one hand on her chest, she used the other to pick up the arrangement. With a look of awe, she stared as if it were a pristine vase full of expensive flowers purchased from the florist. As opposed to what it was, wildflowers from his field gathered in a frenzy on his way to get to her.

In a low voice only for her, he used the words she'd previously said to him. "Everyone deserves fresh flowers."

She looked from the offering to him, her eyes covered in a sheen of tears. "Thank you," she whispered.

The man across from her thrust his hand into Chase's line of vision. "Bob Morton."

Chase clenched his teeth, took a breath and slowly turned to the man. He needed to get a read on the situation. "Chase Cross."

Bob cocked his head and studied him while pumping Chase's hand just a little too hard. "I assume you're related to the gentleman at the bar who said hello to us earlier."

"Hunter. He's my twin brother."

"Ah."

Chase edged his hip onto Lexi's side of the booth. "May I join you?"

She nodded, and he scooted in beside her. Bob's eyes darted from Lexi to him.

Chase looked down at the table and for the first time noticed a pile of stapled papers. The words "Prenuptial Agreement" showed boldly at the top of the first page. His stomach plummeted to his boots. He might already be too late.

Maybe it was time to go get his dog.

But if Lexi didn't want him here, she would have said so. Chase kept his tail rooted in the red vinyl booth and looked at Bob. He nodded to the plate in front of the man. "How do you like your chicken-fried steak? It's the best in the state."

Bob ran his fingertips over his round, balding head. The older gentleman looked fit and well put-together in his polo shirt and khaki pants. Chase even saw the kindness in the eyes behind the bifocals, but that didn't mean he was ready to trust him. "I'm sure it's fine," the man said. "It's not what I normally eat."

Not a surprise. This man had city slicker written all over him. Lexi wasn't from these parts, but somehow she blended well with country life. Her boots weren't as dirty as everyone's native to the area, but she wasn't a shiny new penny, either. Something deep in Chase's gut knew she belonged here, in this community.

He hoped Lexi knew it, too.

Chase laced his hands on the table and asked Bob, "Where are you from?"

"Denver."

"What are you doing in these parts?"

The man flashed a glance at Lexi as if asking for permission, and when she nodded, he said, "I'm an attorney and came to discuss matters of a private nature with Lexi."

"And what kind of advice are you giving Lexi?"

She curled her fingers around Chase's forearm. He didn't know if this was an act of support or a warning. He also didn't care because he wasn't going anywhere.

Bob leaned forward. "All due respect, I'm not sure that's any of your business, Mr. Cross."

Chase picked up the prenuptial agreement and thumbed through it. There seemed to be two copies. One with the name Vance Miller in the groom's space and the other with a blank for the name of presumably a different groom. He still didn't know this guy's angle. "Did you bring these with you today?"

"Yes," Bob said.

"Then it is my business. Because I'm Lexi's fiancé." He cocked his head. "Which is why I'm wondering, you filled in one of these incorrectly and left the name of the groom blank on the other of these documents."

Bob held up his hands in surrender. "I was just trying to walk Lexi through her options. I was just trying to help."

He turned to Lexi. "Options?"

"Mr. Morton came to tell me in person that the will is ironclad." She licked her lips. "There's no way around the required marriage clause. So we began discussing the alternatives."

"What alternatives?"

Looking away, she said, "Vance Miller."

"Well, you're not marrying your ex-fiancé." She said options. There must be more. "What else?"

"And a…" She struggled to get the words out and closed her eyes. "A neutral party who could match me with a safe option."

He kept his voice calm. "I thought I was your safe option."

She looked to him. "After yesterday," she said hesitantly, "I didn't know how you felt. I didn't know…"

Lexi dug her fingers deeper into Chase's arm and looked at him as if pleading him to understand.

He understood. He understood that she didn't see what she thought she saw.

He studied her face and found beauty, vulnerability and a bit of a challenge behind her eyes. He spoke to the lawyer, but didn't take his eyes from hers when he said quietly, "She doesn't need your help, Bob. Or your prenuptial agreement."

She blinked, then exhaled a breath. He could almost feel the tension release from her.

Bob placed his hands on the edge of the table and pushed

himself to sit taller. "Are you saying you're going to marry her?"

Chase glared at the man. "I'm saying she's worth more than your offer to coordinate something between an ex-fiancé who conspired with her mother for the money, or a mail-order groom who could be anybody."

Bob leaned in. "You may not get this, but I'm on her side. My job is to protect her."

That may be, but Bob didn't understand that Chase also considered it his job to protect her.

Bob got up to make his exit and pointed to the papers. "If something changes in the next eleven days, just let me know." With one look toward Chase, then back to Lexi, he said, "You know how to get a hold of me."

Chase's stare followed the man as he passed Hunter. His brother wore what Chase presumed was a matching glare to his own. Bob walked out the front door, right past Duke, who barked furiously at him from the truck, and straight to his flashy car. Once he drove off, Chase looked at Lexi.

She glanced at the flowers, to the stapled papers, back to the flowers, then up to him. "I'm sorry," she whispered, then cast her gaze down to her worrying fingers.

He gently took her chin and tilted her head to look at him. "Why are you sorry?"

"Because I asked you to marry me and then talked to my lawyer about other people. None of this is conventional. And all of it is confusing. I have no idea what to do about any of it. Or why you're even here." She blew out a long breath. "But I'm so relieved to see you, I'm not sure any of it matters."

He nodded, holding her eyes in his.

"Seriously," she continued, her entire demeanor seeping vulnerability, "I don't know why you're here."

"I needed to know what your socks say today."

A short chuckle burst from her mouth. Good. He wanted her to smile.

"They say 'Brave' on them."

"Perfect," he said softly.

"Now. Why are you really here?"

"I'm glad I showed when I did." He nodded to her untouched plate of food. "Every time a plate of chicken-fried steak goes untouched, a cowboy loses his spurs."

"Is that so?" she asked, a giggle in her tone.

He pulled her plate in front of him and cut the steak in half. After leaning over the table to retrieve an extra set of silverware, he unrolled the utensils from their paper napkin and pointed the fork at her. "Dig in."

She stared at him warily, but ate a few bites of the mashed potatoes. Good. He wanted her to eat something and relax.

From across the room, Hunter waved at him on his way out the door. Chase lifted his chin in return. He glanced at Sheila, who stared at his brother with stars in her eyes. Chase was going to have to talk to Hunter about his intentions with the waitress.

For now, he had his hands full with the beautiful, confusing but definitely-worth-fighting-for Lexi Gardner.

"So." She chewed a bite and swallowed. "Are you going to tell me what you're doing here?"

Sheila strolled by their table and set a glass of water in front of Chase. He nodded a thanks to her and took a sip. "I'd like to ask you the same."

"We have other possibilities." She wiped her mouth with her paper napkin and looked at him. "You don't have to marry me."

Thunder rolled through him, and he growled his next words. "You do not have to settle for those possibilities."

She placed her hand on his forearm again, this time gently. "Chase, this solves all our problems. I get married and have access to the trust, which means I can use it for the ranch. And you don't have to do something you promised you would never do again by marrying me."

Confusion hit him square in the chest, along with something painful, yet sweet. "You'd still use your money for the nonprofit?" he asked softly, almost to himself.

"Of course." She squeezed his arm. "I believe in Four Cross Hope, Chase. With everything in my being."

He cleared away the emotion crawling up his throat. He had to stay focused, even if the sweet smell of her shampoo was throwing him off in such close proximity.

"Maybe I don't want an out," he said a little angrier than he intended. He threw his napkin on the table and turned to her. "Maybe I want a shot."

Lexi's brown eyes grew three times in size. She looked as surprised as he felt hearing the words come out of his mouth.

But he wouldn't take them back. He meant them.

"You don't want to get married again." She sputtered her words. "A-and the things your mother-in-law said. Laura was perfect for you. I can't—"

"My former mother-in-law is a good woman. But she didn't know anything about my day-to-day relationship with her daughter. It wasn't always an easy road." He shook his head. His relationship with Laura was one filled with love, but it certainly was not without challenges.

Lexi blinked. Twice.

He turned toward her and ran an arm across the top of the booth behind her. "I have a good time with you when we're actually getting along. Do you have a good time with me?"

Slowly, she looked up at him, her glassy eyes full of emotions he wished he could decipher. "I have a good time with you," she whispered.

He nodded once. "Good. I think we make a good team. Do you think we make a good team?"

Her face flushed pink, and she licked her lips. "Yes. We make a good team."

At her answer, the spot over his heart squeezed. He rubbed the place, but realized the squeeze wasn't painful. It was something he didn't quite recognize. Looking into her beautiful eyes, he said, "I can't make promises, Lexi. But I can tell you that I want to spend the next eleven days figuring this out together. Will you do that with me?"

"Are you sure?"

He hated that she had to ask that question, but he understood why. She deserved clarity.

"You want to know what I'm doing here?" He picked up the prenuptial papers and looked at her. Without breaking eye contact, he ripped them in half. "That's what I'm doing here," he said.

"Oh," she murmured, staring at the torn papers.

He returned his arm to the back of the booth and angled back toward her. When he gently cupped the back of her head, she stared up at him. He leaned in and pressed his lips to her forehead. Pulling back, he asked, "Will you spend the next eleven days figuring this out with me?"

"Yes," she said in a voice so quiet that he barely heard her.

He pressed his lips to her forehead one more time, having no idea what would come of the next eleven days.

Before today, he didn't know if she might change her mind. Now he didn't know if she'd flip-flop again. And he didn't know if they should put money down on this contractor, thus committing her trust fund to the cause and them to marriage.

What he did know was that he was all in to figure out a way to get through this—with her by his side.

Chapter Nine

Pressure. All Chase could feel was pressure. Calving season was in full swing with each ranch hand taking shifts. Lexi seemed to be staying afloat as Tax Day approached, but he knew she was burning the candle at both ends. The contractor wanted an answer about an early start date. The Four Cross Ranch bank account was holding the line, but barely. And Lexi's birthday was a week from tomorrow.

Standing in the lodge, Chase shook his head. A new soldier on leave had arrived this morning. A good thing. But another thing all the same. He didn't dare tell Lexi he was personally absorbing the costs. His savings could handle it. What couldn't handle it was his schedule.

He could feel the exhaustion in his bones.

His phone rang, and when he looked at the screen, he wanted to ignore it. But if Hunter needed him on the ranch, he needed to know. "Hunter," he answered. "Everything okay with that heifer?"

"She's fine. She won't calve again, but we got her stabilized."

Chase closed his eyes and exhaled. It had been a long morning. "Okay."

"You on property?" Hunter asked.

"Just got back from the bank and I'm at the lodge waiting on Lexi."

"You guys married yet?"

He walked to the front of the house and looked for Lexi out the window. He shook his head. His brother knew the answer. "You worried we got married and I didn't ask you to be the best man?"

"I'm worried you're about to mess up the best thing that's come your way in a long time. I don't understand why you're waiting a week."

"Hunter, Lexi's wrapping up tax season, and I'm just trying to survive calving season. Neither of us wants to fall asleep while we're taking our vows."

"You're hedging."

After a long exhale, Chase looked at the ground and lowered his voice. "I'm giving her every chance she needs to make sure this is what she wants to do."

"You're still hedging."

He squeezed his eyes closed, as if he could guard himself from the truth. "What am I supposed to do here? Marry a woman I'm not in love with so I can use her money to make all my dreams come true?"

"I can think of about three things wrong with that question."

Lexi drove up in her old car and slowly pulled herself out of the driver's seat. She looked as tired as he felt. As she grabbed something from the back seat, Chase decided to disregard his brother's last comment. "I've got to go. I'll head to the barn when I'm done."

He hung up before Hunter could say anything else annoying.

Chase opened the front door of the lodge just as Lexi made it to the top of the stairs holding two large grocery sacks. She stopped and her ponytail swayed behind her head. Jeans, a sweatshirt underneath an open coat, tennis shoes, no makeup, dark circles under her brown eyes—and this woman was still beautiful.

He cleared his throat. "Let me take your bags."

"I've got it. If I let go, I might drop them."

He approached her anyway, wrapped his hands around the bottom of the bags and withdrew them from her. Before he got caught in the wildflowers of her scent, he headed into the lodge and set the groceries down on the counter.

They worked in companionable silence putting the food and drinks away for the new guest.

Opening the fridge, she stowed the milk on the inside of the door. "How many hours of sleep did you get last night?"

"A few." He put the last of the cans of food in the pantry.

"My schedule only gets like this once a year. Sometimes quarterly taxes can pick up the pace a little, but it's nothing like April." She drew her arms over her head and stretched out long. "What about you? Is this what life is always like for you?"

"There's nothing like calving season."

She put her arms down and shook them out. "I'm sorry to drop and run, but I've got to see a few clients today to finalize their returns."

"You going to finish on time?"

She smiled. "I always finish on time." She might be trying to look cocky, but she only looked cute to him.

Pulling the keys out of her pocket, she said, "Oh, and fair warning. I'll sleep right through the day after Tax Day. It's a ritual and a necessity."

"Do you need me to bring you food?"

She touched the place above her heart. "Oh, thank you. That's not necessary. I can take care of myself."

On the way out of the kitchen, she stopped at the island.

She ran her fingers over the documents on the counter. "What are these?"

He shoved his hands in the front pockets of his jeans. What an idiot! He shouldn't have left those papers out for her to see. "I turned in new projections to the bank. They're going to get a new appraisal for the ranch."

Slowly, she turned to him. "And reconsider the loan," she said, her tone flat.

He studied her. Nodded. "They might."

After a huff, she closed her eyes and talked to him. "Are you pulling out of this, Chase? My birthday is in a week. I'm under a lot of pressure. I'm exhausted. And I don't have time to figure out if you're playing a game with me."

He took a step toward her, a hint of desperation creeping into his voice. "Lexi, I'm not playing a game." But he was in an impossible position.

Her eyes popped open. She scooped up the papers and held them out to him. "Then what is this exactly?"

He quieted his voice. "I guess I—"

"You guess you what?" she demanded.

"I can't reconcile marrying you for money."

She looked stricken. No. She looked betrayed. Then resigned. "If you don't want to marry me, just tell me now."

"What?" Hunter was right. He was messing up everything. "That's not it."

"It's okay." She started walking toward the front door and opened it. When she turned around, they were face-to-face, a breath apart. "It's okay, Chase. If you don't want to marry me, I get it." She barked a sarcastic laugh. "I promise you that I get it. I just need you to tell me so I can plan otherwise."

He took her hand. "Don't plan otherwise, Lexi. We're doing this."

She swallowed, a cold look on her face, her chin out almost in defiance. "You can tell me. Is it Laura? You don't want to get married again because you lost Laura?"

Was it Laura? He shoved the thought away. "No."

"Just tell me."

What had he done? His stomach clenched tightly. His chest tighter. He schooled his tone and searched her eyes. "I am telling you. You're going to finish tax season, sleep for a day, and then we're getting married."

A tear slipped down her left cheek, and she quickly rubbed it away with her palm. "Okay," she whispered. "Okay."

With one day until Tax Day and five days until Lexi's birthday, relentless knots churned in her stomach. Today, it seemed as though the discomfort was spreading, and it felt like acid coated her insides.

Externally, Wyoming temperatures hinted at warmer days. Internally, pressure from Chase and Lexi's situation had built over the last two and a half weeks and was taking a toll. The clear skies behind the striking Snowy Range couldn't compete with the volcano swirling inside of Lexi.

She pasted a fake smile on her face and rang the Stimpsons' doorbell. Mr. and Mrs. Stimpson were old-school. They wanted their tax return printed, signed and mailed. She just needed to get their signatures. But maybe a visit to the couple at Bright Horizons would also serve as a distraction.

A wreath decorated in wooden flowers greeted her with the words "April Showers Bring May Flowers" scrolled across the top. It shook when the elderly woman answered the door. Upon recognition of Lexi, her face lit up. "Lexi. So good to see you. How are you?"

Lexi tried to widen her smile. "Fine. Fine. I brought you flowers." She thrust the vase forward. Nothing could be done for Lexi. But maybe Mrs. Stimpson's day would brighten from the gentle scent of the calla lilies.

Mrs. Stimpson's brow drew down in concern. "Come in. George is in the back on a call and will come find us when he finishes. You look like you need some lemonade, dear." Apparently, Lexi wasn't fooling anyone.

With careful movements, Lexi shifted to the couch and waited while Mrs. Stimpson chatted about the latest news in the retirement community and prepared the refreshments.

"Apparently Sam Gutton finally asked his sweetheart Myrna Franklin to marry him. They both moved to Bright Horizons after their loved ones died. They've been neighbors for three years. Not one date. And then bam, he popped the question. I can't even imagine the whiplash they must be feeling, going from friends to engaged in no time flat."

"I can kind of imagine it," Lexi muttered to herself.

Mrs. Stimpson leaned her head through the door. "What, dear?"

"Nothing." She swallowed. "It does feel fast."

Very fast.

Mrs. Stimpson returned to the living room and set down a tray. Store-bought sugar cookies were arranged on a stack of paper napkins next to two glasses of lemonade. She perched nearby on the couch and angled her body toward Lexi. A crease ran down the middle of her pressed pants, and her perfectly manicured hands lay together in her lap. "Now. How is that young man of yours. Chase? What is he up to these days?"

"Oh, um." Lexi rubbed a tight spot under her rib. She was thankful she'd worn her looser yoga pants with a long sweater tunic today. Her sensitive stomach couldn't have handled a tight waistband. "Calving season has him pretty busy. One of his brothers didn't come home to help this year like they'd hoped, so they're a man down."

At least that's how Chase's texts explained the situation.

There had been only short texts from him the last two days. Quick check-ins. She wondered if their last conversation upset him as much as it upset her.

The older woman's eyes narrowed, but she said nothing.

The small bite Lexi took from one of the cookies tasted like sandpaper. She washed it down with a sip of lemonade that caused a wave of nausea to run through her. It seemed her nerves weren't going to leave her alone until her birthday passed.

She turned toward the older woman and crossed her ankles. "Mrs. Stimpson, do you mind if I ask you a question?"

"Lexi, every woman my age wishes someone would ask them a question. Especially if they, in turn, get to talk about themselves. Bonus points if they get to give unsolicited advice."

Lexi laughed, but a muscle spasmed in her side. She bit back her wince and asked the question that had been swirling in the middle of her volcano. "Is love supposed to be sacrificial? And if so, what does that look like? And if that's the case, how does anyone ever get what they want if they're all sacrificing things for the sake of love?"

The woman peered at her so long, Lexi began to fear she'd probe further. One simple question might shatter Lexi's hold on her total confusion about where God's love fit into the mess created by the trust.

But Mrs. Stimpson straightened her sweater set and sat back. "Louella said something to me once that stuck. My guess is it's the kind of thing she would have wished she'd passed on to her granddaughter."

Tears hit the back of Lexi's eyes. The burden of the next five days left her with a deep weariness she desperately wished she could share with her grandmother. "What did she say?" she whispered.

Mrs. Stimpson took Lexi's hand in hers and gentled her voice. "She said whatever we think is ours...probably wasn't ever ours to begin with. And that we have to let go of something to know if it was really meant for us."

A sheen of sweat broke out on Lexi's brow. "It's hard to hear that advice considering what happened to my grandmother. She let go of my mother, and my mother never came back to her."

"Yes. But all was not lost." A smile peeked at the edge of Mrs. Stimpson's lips. "*You* came back to her."

"But only for six weeks. Then I lost her."

She nodded. "But I don't think you truly understand. What was meant for her was *you*. Those six weeks she had with you felt like a gift to Louella."

"She said that to you?"

"Many times."

A tear streamed down Lexi's cheek. It wouldn't douse the volcano, but it spread out, filling the cracks of the parched wound her mother had left in her.

No matter how the next five days played out, Lexi never wanted to forget what Mrs. Stimpson shared with her. Lexi was chosen. Maybe not by her mother. Or through a marriage. But she was beloved by a grandmother who needed Lexi just as much as Lexi needed her.

She said whatever we think is ours, probably wasn't ever ours to begin with. And that we have to let go of something to know if it was really meant for us.

Chase's handsome face came to mind. The love for his

family. Their land. Struggling veterans. His vision for the future of Four Cross Hope.

"I'm falling for Chase Cross," Lexi whispered through a sad, watery smile.

"I thought that might be the case," Mrs. Stimpson said quietly.

"But I don't think he was meant for me." Something tore in Lexi's heart. "I might have been meant for him, but I don't think he was meant for me."

Question filled the lines of the wise woman's face. "Are you sure about that?"

"No." She pictured Chase's fierce fear after the incident with the snake. "But I can't ask him to *make* himself be meant for me. That's not fair to either of us."

With no more wisdom from Mrs. Stimpson, Lexi received signatures from both Stimpsons. After a kind good-bye and heartfelt hugs, she left Bright Horizons.

When she got in her car, she checked her cell phone. Two texts and one voicemail. Caller ID said the voicemail was from her lawyer. She listened to it first.

"Hi, Lexi. I just wanted to follow up with our meeting last week and let you know that I talked to my buddy who's a judge. He shut me down pretty fast. There's just no way around the wording of the will. You must be married by your thirty-fifth birthday to gain access to the trust. Otherwise, I'll be contacting your second cousin who, by the way, is still married as of today. I checked county courthouse records." A heavy sigh came through the recording. "I'm sorry. I know that's not the news you were hoping for. Keep me posted."

Nausea swept over her. This time worse than the last.

She'd known this would probably be her lawyer's answer.

But why was her car so hot? And how come her body felt like it had run to Yellowstone and back?

She turned the engine over and aimed the air vents at herself full speed. Just those movements seemed to make her winded.

When she scrolled through her phone, the texts she found stoked the fire in her volcano. The first was from her mother.

Your birthday's in five days. I've found us an option. He'll split the money three ways. Call me. You are running out of time.

The text spiked a pain in her side. Of course her mother was still angling for the money. What did she mean she'd found an option? Was she trying to partner Lexi with Vance again? Or this time was it a complete stranger?

Lexi would always miss her mother. Miss what could have been. Miss the relationship she wished it had been. But she could never trust her again.

And the more she thought about the money, the sicker she became to her stomach.

She read Chase's text next.

I know tomorrow's deadline day for you. I think I can get away for dinner tonight if you want me to bring takeout to your house. We need to talk.

Chase was a good guy. A solid man.

She placed her phone on the passenger seat, gripped the top of the steering wheel and pressed her forehead into the back of her hands. Her gut roiled and her body was wracked with shivers.

Lexi never wanted to be the reason behind the pain in

Chase's eyes. She never wanted to be the cause of the debilitating fear she saw in him after she was almost thrown from Millie. And she couldn't ask him to be a different man. She wouldn't want him to be.

Is this what falling for someone felt like? Surely that wasn't what was happening. She'd promised him their marriage would be based on a logical decision. An exchange. But she had the feeling she wasn't going to be able to keep that promise.

"Maybe I've gotten everything wrong in the past," she whispered, "but I know what I need to do now."

She sat up, brushed the remnants of her tears off her hot cheeks and aimed her car toward her house. She'd finish her work tomorrow, bypass sleeping for a little longer, and then have a talk with Chase.

Chapter Ten

Chase's phone taunted him.

Only three minutes had passed since the last time he checked. No texts. No calls. Nothing from Lexi.

The woman was supposed to be at the ranch forty-five minutes ago. He'd reached out to her repeatedly, but she never replied.

The sun hung low somewhere in the sky, not that Chase had paid any attention to it for weeks. Neither did the calving cows. Their babies came when they were good and ready and had zero regard for the time of day or night. Weariness was in the soil. It felt like no one was getting any sleep this year.

He took his hat off and wiped his forehead with the back of his arm.

Hunter sidled up to him. "You going to talk about it or just make the rest of us around you miserable?"

Chase grumbled, "You going to banish me to shoeing the horses?"

"I wouldn't take a job from the farrier." He turned to Chase and crossed his arms. "But I might send you to KP duty just to get you off the land. You're making the cows cranky."

"The cows are cranky because they just gave birth. I hear it's not an easy task."

Chase turned from his brother. He leaned his weight into his forearms on top of the split-rail fence and aimed his eyes at the back of the chow hall where Lexi should emerge any second.

Hunter mirrored his stance next to him, but said nothing. Which meant he wasn't leaving until Chase gave him something.

On a sigh, Chase finally said, "The bank called."

"Hmm," was all Hunter replied.

"In spite of the new numbers and projections I gave them earlier this week, they turned us down again." He had even thrown in details about possible donors, but without concrete evidence of procured future funding, the bank couldn't make the loan. Even if the manager went to high school with him and knew the Cross family's upstanding reputation.

The muscles in Chase's shoulders felt like rocks. Heavy, sedentary stress tightened just a bit more each time he thought of the ranch, the trust and Lexi.

He was torn about sharing the bank's rejection with Lexi. He didn't want to put more pressure on the situation. Because he couldn't secure the loan, the need for money walked a tightrope stretched taut between Lexi and him.

"Three days until Lexi's birthday," Chase murmured.

Hunter grunted.

His twin wasn't going to bail him out of the conversation. Typical. The man would throw himself in front of a train for him. He was loyal, almost to a fault. Had sacrificed his late twenties to raise their siblings. And Chase never knew how to compete with a man of that honor.

"What made you leave the military and go home to take care of Cora and Ryder?" The question had been festering between the twins for over a decade.

Hunter shooed a fly away from his face and settled back into the fence. "It's what was needed to be done."

Chase turned to his brother and leaned against the wooden rail. "But you'd dreamed of being in the military your whole life. We both did."

Turning his head, Hunter looked at Chase. "The family needed me."

"It was a huge sacrifice," Chase said, his tone perplexed. He just stared at his brother. His volume rose. "Why aren't you angry at me for not leaving the military with you? Don't you have regrets?"

Hunter shook his head as if he couldn't believe the questions Chase was firing at him. He squared his body to him and said in a disbelieving tone, "Chase, you seem to think that sacrifices can only lead to hardship."

Chase's entire body jerked back at his brother's confusing comment.

"I'm not saying it was easy to come home—" Hunter looked over his shoulder at the land "—but it doesn't feel like a sacrifice anymore because too much good came from it. Especially now."

"What do you mean?"

"In spite of everything that's happened to her, Cora's finding her way. There's something good and solid about getting to see that up close." He threw a hand out. "And Ryder—"

"Ryder's a piece of work."

A smile hitched at the corner of Hunter's mouth. "I'm not nearly as concerned about Ryder as I am about you."

"That's saying a lot."

Hunter nodded once. "How's Lexi feeling?"

"What do you mean?"

"Sheila told me Lexi went by the diner earlier today and didn't look good."

She wouldn't. Her birthday was in three days. Maybe she was as wound-up as Chase was, trying to figure out how their situation was going to end. Calving and tax seasons could not have come at a worse time. He and Lexi hadn't had near the time together he had hoped heading into this week.

He looked out over the land, his horse grazing in the distance.

Who was he kidding? The incident with Mildred had freaked him out. Chase was more skittish than the horse. That snake had bitten him with a healthy dose of reality.

Caring for another woman would cost him something, and he wasn't sure if he had the means to pay.

But he cared for Lexi. Deeply. There wasn't anything he could do about it.

He rubbed the spot on the left side of his chest. The one that had plagued him constantly for weeks.

A car drove by in the distance, but it wasn't Lexi's heap. "She was supposed to come by for dinner—" he checked his phone for the twenty-third time this hour "—but she's late. Really late."

"Makes sense. Sheila said it looked like Lexi could barely move." Hunter scrubbed the stubble at his cheek. "Maybe she didn't make it here because she couldn't."

Chase could barely hear Hunter's last words as he ran to his truck.

Chase held the phone to his ear, simultaneously pounding on Lexi's door.

Her car was in her driveway but parked at a funny angle. He'd been standing at the door for three full minutes knocking. He was now putting his body weight into his fist to create a louder noise.

In the meantime, she wasn't answering her phone.

Fear.

Raw, unadulterated fear coursed through his veins.

He spun around and walked along the side of her house, peering in the windows. All the curtains were drawn. Something she told him she did to cut down on energy costs as the weather turned warmer. Pure Lexi.

Pure Lexi.

That spot on his chest burned.

The back door was locked. As he stormed off the porch, he knocked over a potted plant. Spilling out of the dirt was a rock. But something didn't look quite right about it.

He crouched down and realized it was a hide-a-key rock. Relief hit him as he slid the key out and proceeded to open her back door.

"Lexi?" he called as he bounded through the kitchen. "Lexi, it's me. Chase. Are you here?"

A low moan came from the living room, and he rushed through the swinging door to the sound.

Styrofoam take-out boxes were strewn across her rug, the contents next to Lexi's dumped purse. And phone.

Curled in a ball on her denim couch, Lexi's body shook. Her eyes were squinted closed, and terrible pain struck through her pale face.

His heart lurched in his chest, pulling him to sit on the edge of the couch beside her pain-wracked body.

"Honey?" A layer of sweat covered her face. He moved to touch her forehead, but he could feel the heat coming off her even before the back of his hand made contact. "Honey, you're burning up."

When he placed his hand on her waist, she cried out. A dreadful sound that jolted him back.

He scanned her body, looking for any hint of injury. "What else hurts, honey?"

"Mmm." She swallowed but didn't open her eyes.

He gently shifted damp bangs off her forehead. "Can you talk to me?"

She licked her lips and whispered, "Nauseated."

Nausea. Fever. Painful to touch. She needed to get to a hospital.

"Honey, you need to see a doctor."

"No," she moaned. A sob broke through, causing a fierce wince, clearly so painful for her to endure that tears streamed down her face.

Her guttural sound broke something in him. The entire picture of her ripped his heart out of his chest.

"Come on, honey." Trying his best not to jostle her, he bent low at the knees and scooped her into his arms.

She constricted as if she could brace against the pain, then her head lolled against his chest. The heat from her body radiated against his like nothing he'd ever experienced.

Should he throw her into a cold bath? But what if something was wrong internally? Delaying medical treatment could be fatal.

The responsibility for her life robbed him of his next breath. Almost debilitated him.

She shifted in his arms and curled into him, shivers bucking her entire body. "Chase," she whispered against his neck, her voice croaking. "I'm s-sorry."

His legs found their footing and he strode to the front door, leaning down to unlock it and walk through.

When he got her situated in the front seat, he texted

Hunter, Headed to hospital with Lexi, and pointed his car in the direction of help.

He held her hand. He wanted to squeeze it. To reassure her that everything was going to be okay.

But he didn't want to hurt her.

And he didn't know if everything was going to be okay.

And Lexi pitifully…painfully…murmured his name the entire drive to the emergency room. Followed by the word *sorry*.

Devastating heat.

Scorching pain in her side.

Chase.

Oh, no. Chase.

She was sorry. She was so sorry he had to see her like this. That he had to deal with her in this state.

His wife.

His heart.

Her Chase.

Blackness. Finally—a beautiful black that took away her pain.

But it also took away her Chase.

Because when she woke up in the recovery room, with machines beeping, effective pain medication and a nurse who reassured her that she was fortunate they caught the ruptured appendix when they did, there was no Chase to be found.

Chapter Eleven

~✎~

Chase lay in the only spot in the world where he knew he could breathe. Out on his land. In the wide-open spaces. But now, Laura's mountain was in plain view. With Laura's memory at the edge of his sanity. With Laura's death searing into him through Lexi's broken body.

Once he'd heard Lexi had made it out of surgery all right, he'd bolted from the hospital.

Sleep was not his friend, followed by a frenzied day on the ranch tracking down two calves, the veteran leaving the lodge, rounding up cattle from a fence break, and one breech-birth calf delivery Chase had handled himself. All while picturing Lexi's pained, pale face coupled with the words the doctor described of an excruciating surgery to clean up her ruptured appendix.

He'd known he should go see her. He'd called himself all kinds of names throughout the day, the word *coward* on repeat in his head. The fear of losing Lexi froze him with a white heat he'd never known. The hospital walls had suffocated him the night before. He couldn't go back.

By the end of the day, in an almost unhinged daze, he had saddled up Harvey and rode through his land. As acres and acres passed beneath him, he hoped the horse's hooves could pound out the pain in his chest. Could pound out the fear that refused to leave his bloodstream even though he knew intellectually that Lexi was okay. Could pound out the reality that he couldn't fathom that he almost lost someone else that he loved.

Because he loved Lexi. In the most terrifying, complete way. He loved Lexi.

He loved Alexis Jane Gardner, and he had no idea if he could handle loving her.

Which was what he was thinking about when on the unseasonably warm April night, he finally fell into a fitful sleep in the grass by his favorite part of the fence line, a direct line of sight to his mountain.

But that wasn't what he was thinking about when he felt a slobbery, scratchy tongue lick his cheek and smelled the unmistakable breath of a canine.

Chase gently shoved the whiskery face away from his and squinted with one eye open at his dog. "Duke."

His golden retriever's body shook with urgency.

"Your dog wants to know why you aren't at the hospital with Lexi," Hunter said, towering over Chase and blocking the early sun's rays.

"That's probably truer than you know," muttered Chase as he sat up, his bones groaning at him about being too old to sleep on the hard floor of the ranch lands.

Hunter's voice lowered with a tone he rarely used and only when he was upset with someone. "What are you doing out here, Chase?"

He cocked his legs and rested his elbows on his knees. A sigh came from deep in his chest. "I don't know."

Hunter looked toward the mountain, then back to Chase. "At some point, you're going to have to trust God with Laura. She wasn't ever yours to begin with. She was always His."

"And she died, Hunter." Chase tried to rein in his anger.

He swiped at a bug on his arm. "What kind of a pep talk is this? Because I don't think you're very good at it."

"The kind where you get it straight in your head that Lexi isn't yours, either."

The words felt like a sucker punch.

His brother added, "And you're going to have to trust God with her whether you like it or not."

The second sucker punch packed more heat than the first one.

Chase scratched at the stubble on his face. "What if I can't?"

Duke barked his own rebuke at him as if he knew what the conversation was about.

"Tough," Hunter lectured. "You will. You'll do it every day because fear can't drive your decisions. You'll do it every day because there are no guarantees. And you'll do it every day because that's the choice we get. To trust God with the things that were His to begin with."

Chase eyed his dog. Then his brother. "That's not a fun set of truths, Hunter."

"Each day is in God's hands, whether we like it or not."

Chase roughed his fingers through his hair several times. He inhaled oxygen from his land. From his heritage.

"I love her," he said quietly to the ground.

"I know. But this problem's not a hard riddle to solve, Chase." Hunter crossed his arms. "Marry her."

Chase squinted up at his brother. "It's not that simple."

"Why not?"

"If I marry her now, she'll always question if it was about the money." He shook his head. "I can't do that to her. I can't let the woman I marry always wonder in the back of her mind if I did it for any reason other than that I treasure her and don't want to live the rest of my life without her. There should be no doubt in her mind. She deserves nothing less."

But her birthday loomed in front of them. In about seventeen hours, give or take a few minutes, she would turn thirty-five.

Hunter nodded, bent to slap him on the shoulder, looked in his eyes and said, "You'll figure it out." He extended a hand and helped Chase off the ground.

"That's it?" Chase laughed humorlessly. "You've spent the last month with so much advice about Lexi, I think you're out of your word allotment for the year. But now? Now that it's down to the wire, all you can say is that I'll figure it out?"

"And that you need to take a shower."

"Unbelievable."

With a grin, Hunter tipped his hat, said no more and sauntered back in the direction of the lodge.

Chase shook his head. He could not wait until some woman knocked Hunter off his feet. Couldn't happen to a better man.

Duke jumped several times and barked orders to Chase. He ran three steps in the direction of the lodge, then looked back and barked again. Three steps toward Chase, a bark. Then three steps toward the lodge.

Or maybe the parking lot.

It was as if his dog knew Chase was late getting to Lexi.

"I know, buddy." He rubbed his hands down his dog's excited body. "Don't worry. We're going to get her. She may not want me after the stunt I pulled leaving her, but we're going to try."

After an attempt at dusting off his hopelessly dirty jeans, Chase paused to look toward his mountain. Its strength could not be denied, but the white clouds at the summit made him think the peak was tucked into Heaven.

"What do you want from me?" he asked the mountain. Maybe he was asking his wife. Definitely he was asking God.

"I want to trust You with Lexi, Lord," he whispered. "And I want to marry her."

A soft breeze swept over him, bringing a peace with its gentle touch. And the very distinct feeling that while he was staring at his mountain, somehow, someway, it had shifted a little. Created space. Given him room to breathe. And allowed him to leave his wife in the hands of the Lord. On the mountain. Where she belonged.

Which allowed him to leave to be by Lexi's side. At the hospital. Maybe for forever. Where he belonged.

Lexi's body woke in stages.

Only her ears worked at first.

The beeps of a machine. Nearby rustling. And the low murmurs of voices.

Next, she could smell. Something metallic. A heavy cleaning product. A woman's perfume.

Prying her eyes open proved to be a bigger feat than she thought it would be. She could open them for a second, the room would focus, then blur, then she'd close them again.

Once again. But this time, the face of a woman in her view.

Did she call her mom?

No. She didn't. But she had asked the nurse to call her mom.

Because Chase had left her side.

The beeping machine next to her bed told her that thinking about Chase leaving her did not sit well. Her heartbeat had quickened. Probably because it was too broken to beat regularly when it thought about the cowboy. But she had to convince her heart this was for the best.

She couldn't ask Chase to be someone he was not. She couldn't ask him to love her. She never should have approached him to begin with.

So now, she'd have to marry someone else. Was there time for that?

Chase would be free to live in the memory of his wife, without the fear of losing someone else. Lexi would ask her lawyer for help contacting the neutral party to match her with someone. She would still put her half of the trust money toward Four Cross Hope, and Chase would get everything he wanted in life.

Because that's what love did.

She opened her eyes again. This time for longer.

Her mother held her hand.

When Lexi opened her mouth, it felt unpleasant. She ran her tongue over the back of her teeth. Did someone give her sawdust to chew? "Thirsty," she barely croaked out.

Her mom picked up a cup and pointed its straw toward her mouth. "Just take sips at first. Your body has been through a lot."

Lexi did as she was told. The cool water slid down her sore throat. She coughed, and her mom placed a hand behind her shoulders to move her forward. But pain shot through her side, and she winced at the movement.

"Sorry," her mother murmured. "The nurse wanted to know when you woke up. I'll go get her."

When her mother left to grab a nurse, Lexi leaned back, discouraged that two sips of water made her feel like she'd ridden a bull.

Her mother returned with a middle-aged nurse whose

beautiful black hair streaked with white matched perfectly with the wisdom behind her experienced eyes. "Good morning, sleeping beauty. I'm Julie, your nurse." She checked Lexi's vitals and tapped information into an iPad. "We didn't quite know when you would wake up. Do you remember anything that happened?"

"Someone told me I had surgery but was fine."

"A pretty nasty ruptured appendix. We're keeping you a few days to pump you with antibiotics, but you'll make a full recovery."

Lexi looked around the room trying to orient herself with her situation. The dry-erase board caught her eye. The date had to be wrong. "What day is it?"

The blood-pressure cuff around Lexi's arm tightened. Her stomach did the same when she saw her mother's expression. It was a terrible cross between concerned and conflicted.

The cuff ticked tighter.

The nurse laughed. "Don't worry. We all saw your birthday on your chart. You didn't miss it. It's tomorrow."

"Tomorrow?" She'd slept through an entire day? Lexi tried to push to sit up further, but her side protested. She grimaced. "Tomorrow?"

"Well," the nurse said to the IV bag, thumping the drip chamber, "technically, your birthday is in about twelve hours."

Dread coursed through her veins along with whatever the nurse was giving her. It was noon. On the eve of her birthday. There was no time to find a different husband.

Before her appendicitis, she thought she knew what she wanted. But she also thought she had a few days to think about it. Let it settle.

Twelve hours?

A sharp rap sounded, followed immediately by some-one opening the door. It was strange to recognize a person simply by the way they knocked on a door, but the effi-ciency of the rap, not asking if they could enter and the whip of the privacy curtain aside only confirmed what she already knew.

Vance stood just inside the room. "Lexi."

At least the man knew enough not to approach her.

"How did you…" Lexi didn't know what to say. Again, the sounds on her heart monitor sped up and alerted the room to how Lexi felt about her ex-fiancé's arrival.

Her mother stepped forward. "I called him, Lexi."

"Hey, sweetheart," he said.

His endearment made her stomach clench. Or maybe it was the aftermath of the surgery.

A breath rushed out of her mouth. The money. "Of course you contacted Vance," she whispered.

Her mother, dressed in a champagne-colored pantsuit, folded her hands in front of her. "When the nurse called, she used your maiden name. I know you're not married. I know your birthday is tomorrow. And I know what's at stake. You don't want to lose all of that money."

Vance sat in front of her in a designer suit.

Maybe he came from work.

Or maybe he thought today was their wedding day.

Vance lowered his voice. "Lex. Think about this. You know me. It's not just that I could help, but that we could be the family we always talked about becoming." His eyes pleaded with her to understand. "My parents are here. Just in case you say yes. We all want this."

"Um…" Lexi's brain couldn't catch up. Mortified, she cov-ered her face with her hands, dragging the IV tube across her body in the process. "Vance," she said in an agonized tone.

Too many things were happening in the room. Every girl wanted her mom to take care of her when she was sick. It was probably why she'd told the nurse to call her. But the woman before her? The woman who schemed to get her married off and take money from the trust? The woman who'd barely talked to her for almost two years until recently when her thirty-fifth birthday was hanging over them?

She wasn't sure she wanted that version of Clara Gardner in the room.

Vance turned and squared off with her mother but continued to speak to Lexi, his voice louder and more firm than before. "I have no intention, however, of giving your mother a portion of the trust fund."

Lexi's heart monitor sounded like a fire station alarm. She looked at Julie. "Can you please turn that off?"

"Your pulse has gone to concerning levels three times in the last ten minutes. I think we need to keep you monitored, all things considered."

She had no idea.

Her mother stepped to the foot of her bed. "Lexi, this isn't what you think."

"After last time, what is she supposed to think?" Vance said, using a harsh tone she'd never heard from him before.

Her mother's body stood stiff, and Lexi's blood-pressure cuff tightened again.

Every neuron in Lexi's brain had been firing on all cylinders to try to keep up with the events in the room. But at Vance's words, it was as if they all came to a complete halt. She turned her head to him. "After what happened last time with *you*, what am I supposed to think?"

"You're supposed to think—" Vance snapped his mouth closed. Then said quietly, "That I'm marrying you tonight."

"You're marrying him tonight?" a new voice said from the door.

A voice new to some people in the room, but a voice that Lexi recognized unequivocally.

Chase stepped from behind the curtain. "The door was open," he murmured, his eyes never leaving Lexi's.

The ticking cuff released Lexi's arm with a hiss, and the blood-pressure machine beeped wildly.

She only had a few seconds to take in his pressed jeans, starched white shirt, and the flowers in his hand. The look in his eyes held such confusion and vulnerability, her heart squeezed painfully.

"Who are you?" her mother snapped.

Chase's eyes narrowed, and he took in everyone in the room. He looked at Lexi. "I'm her fiancé." Ignoring the collective gasp, he asked, "You doing okay?"

Her heart squeezed again, this time with longing. In spite of the scene Chase walked into, he wasn't concerned with anyone in the room but her. She wanted to block everyone else out and stay in the zone of his words. Just the two of them. But her heart couldn't take it. Her heart remembered who was in the room. Her heart remembered how messed up everything in her life had become and how it had all congregated in the last twenty minutes at the foot of her hospital bed.

Chase glanced behind him. With a perplexed look, he scooted farther into the room and made space for the next person to enter.

The older gentleman, also dressed in a suit, looked at everyone and stated, "Beckett Gentry at your service. Did someone call for a pastor?" He looked at Lexi, the lines in his face full of confusion.

"I didn't call for you, Pastor Gentry," she said, "but it's always good to see you."

"I did," Vance said, and everyone twisted their necks to look at him.

The preacher smiled kindly at her. "Normally, I get called into hospital rooms for somber reasons. But this time, I got called to perform a wedding." He looked at each man. "So, which one of you is the lucky groom?"

Lexi's monitor beeped wildly as if it couldn't take the stress anymore either.

"Okay," the nurse said in a tone that made it clear she was not to be messed with. "We have a patient, nurse, pastor, mother and two possible grooms in this room, which is four too many people. Everyone out."

"But you don't understand," her mother pleaded. "In less than twelve hours—"

"Everyone." Nurse Julie did not break eye contact with her mother. "Out."

After a few seconds of silence, the awkward shuffling began.

Her mother threw a glare at Chase, then eyed Vance. When she looked at Lexi, she said, "For what it's worth, I didn't understand exactly what I was walking into." She swallowed and took a breath. Her tone gentled and the features in her face softened. "I'm glad that the surgery went well and that you're doing better."

The heart monitor and blood-pressure machine would like to debate those words, but Lexi kept her mouth shut. No matter what, she needed to hear that her mother was concerned about her health. As opposed to being concerned about her marital status or trust fund.

"I'll be outside," her mother said before she left the room.

Vance sighed. He rubbed the back of her hand with his. "I'm sorry, Lex. I—"

"With all due respect," Nurse Julie said, "I didn't kick everyone out so you could stay and have a conversation with my patient. She needs rest. And she needs it now."

His shoulders dropped, and he released a long sigh. "I'll be in the waiting room."

In the waiting room. Waiting. To know if they'd get married or not. While she waited in her hospital room, wondering the same thing.

The pastor looked at Lexi and gave her a kind smile. "I'm going to step out. If you need a listening ear, I won't be far."

With everyone exiting, Lexi lost track of Chase. He must have left without saying goodbye.

Again.

She looked at her hands and shook her head. He was the only one she wanted to talk to. But he was also the only one who she shouldn't talk to. She knew where he stood, and she wasn't going to put pressure on him.

Except she heard murmuring on the other side of the privacy curtain. And then Chase stepped around it, standing square to her.

Julie cleared her throat in a way that told Chase she was not pleased.

"One moment, ma'am," he said to the nurse.

He walked the flowers to Lexi's table and set them down. There must have been fifty white daisies in the stunning arrangement. He held Lexi's eyes in his. "Because everyone deserves fresh flowers."

"Chase, I—"

He ran his finger down her cheek. "I'm here if you need me," he whispered. "And I'm here even if you don't need me."

Chase walked out of her hospital room into the lion's

den of another possible groom, a preacher, a pair of her ex-fiancé's parents, and her mother.

Lexi stayed in her room of solitude and impossible questions.

She wasn't sure which of them had it worse. She only knew that she wished he was with her.

Chapter Twelve

Ortho

One nap, a doctor visit, six hours and seven denied requests to speak to her later, Lexi heard the knock at her door and cringed.

How anyone got rest while checked into a hospital, she didn't know, but her situation seemed to exacerbate the problem.

Nurse Julie threw the privacy curtain aside. "Dinnertime."

"Anything good?"

"Most of it looks okay, but if I were you, I'd hoard the graham crackers." She leaned in and shared as if she were spilling state secrets. "The maternity ward denies it, but they've been known to steal our box for their mommas in labor."

Lexi chuckled, then looked at her food and sobered. "I'm not sure I have an appetite."

"Well, we need you to eat, so we can check successful digestion off your list before we release you. But your situation out in the waiting room makes even my insides a little queasy, and I'm known for having an iron stomach." She took Lexi's cup and filled it with water. "Your fan club keeps growing out there."

Lexi started to tear the wrapper off a cracker but froze. "Who else could be out there?"

The nurse gave her a little smile. "Hunter Cross and the Stimpsons."

This stopped Lexi. She cocked her head. "Do you know everyone?"

"When you work in a small hospital, you get to know a lot of the families in neighboring counties." Julie grinned. "I hadn't had the pleasure of meeting you yet but have been told by three people to ask you for help on my taxes."

"I wonder why they're all here," Lexi said, trying again to pull the plastic apart on the wrapper.

"I'm not sure. But I get the feeling they're here for you." Julie leaned in, took the package from her and ripped it open with ease. "*Just* for you. When and if you're ready."

When and if she was ready.

Lexi put a cracker in her mouth but didn't taste it. She chewed mechanically and swallowed it down with a sip of water. The entire process felt laborious, but not because she'd been sick.

It seemed her body wasn't going to cooperate until she dealt with the crowd in the waiting room and all that came with them.

She took a fortifying breath and said, "Will you please ask Vance to come into the room?"

Nurse Julie had been in the middle of checking her IV, but stopped, moving only her eyes to Lexi. "Vance?"

"Yes, please."

The woman's eyes darted back to the numbers on the IV machine, and then she nodded. "Okay," she said. She turned and took three steps, but at the door, she angled back to Lexi. "But if you need anything—" she lowered her voice "—and I mean *anything*, you press the call button."

At the thought of having her personal bouncer just one room away, Lexi smiled. "Thank you."

With a whoosh of the door, Vance rushed to Lexi's side. His hair was disheveled, and he had removed his tie. "Sweetheart. Lex. How are you?"

And with the sound of the pet names Vance used to call Lexi, she knew what she had to do.

She pushed her tray to the side, stalling while she mulled over her words. "Vance, thank you for coming."

His alert eyes sharpened. "Of course I came. How are you feeling?"

"I'm better." She offered him a gracious smile. "At least, I'll be better once we pass midnight."

"Right." He gave her a curt nod and paced at the side of her bed. "Pastor Gentry stayed. So he can perform the ceremony."

"Vance—"

"There's an elderly couple in the waiting room who say they're your friends. I figure we can use them as best man and maid of honor." He frowned. "Though, those two are married, so she'd be the matron of honor."

He was rambling. He always rambled when he was nervous.

"Vance—"

He put his hands out. "And I know things aren't well with your mother, but I think you'd regret it if she wasn't at your wedding. So I've been trying to build a bridge between us."

"Vance," she said with more force.

He clamped his mouth shut and stared at her, his eyes part guarded and part hopeful.

"I can't do this," she said softly.

Placing his hands on his hips, his shoulders drooped, and he bowed his head to look at the ground. "Don't do this, Lex."

"Please come sit next to me." She pointed to the chair beside the bed. "I need to say a few things."

His position remained the same, and he shook his head at the floor. "Please don't do this, Lexi."

The room was so quiet, it was the first time today that she missed the sounds of the heart monitor. Anything to break up the tension.

Lexi gathered her thoughts as moments passed. But time now felt different to Lexi. With her impending birthday, time had been unkind, the unknown ticking its pressure through her life for months. Years.

But as she took a breath and released it, she knew she had found peace with her decision. Time was no longer scary to Lexi.

After Vance sat in the chair at the side of her bed, he took her hand in both of his and rubbed the top of it with his thumbs.

Gently, Lexi said, "I can't marry you, Vance."

He nodded and continued to stroke the top of her hand.

"Can you look at me, please?"

He obliged, but his face held pain, letting her know her request wasn't an easy one.

"I can't marry you because that's not fair to you." He took a breath to say something, but she continued. "I'm in love with someone else."

That stopped him cold. Recognition crossed his face. "The guy in the waiting room."

"But he's not in love with me," Lexi said. "So, it doesn't matter from that standpoint. Except that it's not fair to marry you when I love someone else."

After one final run of his thumbs across her hand, Vance released his hold on her. He sat back and studied her.

"Someone once told me that I deserved to marry a person who treasured me." Lexi stared at her bare left hand, then looked at her ex-fiancé. "And the same is true for you. You need to marry someone who treasures you, Vance."

"Maybe. But what are you going to do about the money?"

"I'm going to let it go."

She took in her first full breath in four weeks. Maybe in two years.

Something struggled behind his eyes. "How can you just let it go?"

Two days ago, she might have considered marrying Vance so she could claim the trust money. But the closer she got to her birthday, the more she understood something with increasing clarity as the seconds ticked away. She took a breath. "Because it wasn't ever mine to begin with."

Frozen in the wake of her words, Vance stared at her.

"Now," Lexi said with a definitive tone, hoping to pull Vance out of his stupor, "will you please ask my mother to come in here?"

"I'm staying, Lex," he said, his voice firm as he stood. "I'm staying in the waiting room until midnight in case you change your mind."

"But you won't stay after midnight, Vance." She could feel the sad smile forming at her lips. She whispered, "And that should be more concerning to you than letting the money go."

Shaking his head, Vance left her room, giving Lexi only a few moments to recover from one tough conversation and prepare for the next.

She smoothed out the top blanket of her covers and heard her mother's high heels clap against the linoleum floor before she actually saw her mother's face.

But the confident sound of her shoes couldn't cover her mother's uncomfortable demeanor. Clara Gardner stood at the end of the bed, fidgeting with her hands and looking everywhere but at her daughter.

"Mom?" Lexi called. "Everything okay?"

"I should be—" She swallowed. "I should be asking you that."

Lexi stayed quiet.

"At least—" her mom threw a hand in the direction of the lobby "—that's what a certain Mrs. Patricia Stimpson just said to me."

"Mrs. Stimpson?"

"Yes." Her mother looked like a child who had been scolded. "It seems Patricia knew Louella and had plenty to say to me."

"I think they were close," Lexi said quietly, not knowing how this conversation was going to go. Patricia Stimpson was never one to bridle her thoughts. She only guessed the woman had given her mother a piece of her mind. It almost made her pity her mother.

"Could I please—" Her mother closed her eyes and shook her head. "What I mean is, would it be okay if I came and sat next to you?"

"Yes." Lexi shifted in her bed to angle toward the chair that Vance had just occupied.

Once her mother sat, she clasped her hands together and instead of looking at Lexi, she spoke to her lap. "We grew up poor."

Lexi remained quiet.

"I had no skills. No education. And the only way I knew how to get out of my situation was to marry someone who could provide for me. I realize that's not a popular thought in this day and age where women can do anything, but it's all I could wrap my brain around."

"And the trust?"

"Louella was your father's mother, and I had no right to that money. But when your father died, I was hurled back to my family roots. I didn't cope well." A sheen of tears hit her mother's eyes. "I know what I did was wrong. That trust has always been yours. I should have let it alone."

Lexi wasn't sure what the future would look like with her mother, but this conversation felt promising.

"Mom, you have to let go of the trust," she whispered.

"I know."

"No. You don't. I mean, you really have to let go of the trust. I'm not getting married tonight."

Abruptly, her mother stood, her chair screeching back a few inches. "What are you talking about?"

"I let Vance go," Lexi said in a calm voice.

Squinching her eyes closed, her mother shook her head quickly several times. "That's probably the right thing to do."

Confused, Lexi studied her mother. "Why the change of heart?"

"Let's just say that being estranged from your daughter for two years is a pain I can't put into words." She wiped a tear off her cheek. "But the second you get a call that your daughter's in surgery, it rights your world back to where it belonged in the first place."

"Mom," Lexi whispered, the lump in her throat almost painful. She wasn't quite sure what to think.

"And what about that other young man in the lobby?" her mother asked.

"What other young man?"

"The one with the twin."

Chase.

Lexi's heart flipped at the thought of the man with the twin.

"He doesn't love me, Mom." She picked up another package of crackers and mashed the contents into pieces. "I'm not going to marry someone who doesn't love me. I deserve more. And so does he."

Her mother hitched a hip out and her entire demeanor changed with full-on attitude and authority. "And just how do you know what he thinks?"

Lexi threw the annihilated cracker package on the dinner tray. "Because he told me."

"Really?" Her mom's entire body bristled. "Because that man asked me for your hand in marriage not an hour ago."

Lexi looked toward the door as if Chase was going to walk through at any minute. "What?" she whispered.

"Yes, ma'am." Her mother yanked her jacket down straight. "Now, what do you think about that?"

He asked her mother for her hand in marriage?

Of course he had. He was the most honorable man Lexi knew. If he was going to marry someone, arranged or otherwise, he would ask the parents for their daughter's hand in marriage.

If Lexi's heart was on the monitor right now, it would spike off the charts.

Only...

She still couldn't marry him.

He was doing it as a favor to her. Forcing himself to morph into something she needed for the trust.

Even if the money could accomplish great things for his nonprofit, marrying Lexi would sacrifice who Chase was. And she couldn't do that to the man she loved.

"Will you please send Hunter Cross into my room?"

Her mother's head reared back. "Hunter? Chase's twin?"

Once Lexi convinced her mother to send in the correct twin, she waited.

She was doing the right thing. She knew it. Right things

didn't always feel good when you were doing them, so she ignored the way her heart hurt.

Hunter entered the room and stood a few feet from her bed. He crossed his arms over his vast chest, but said nothing.

Lexi looked out the window, watching the sun go down on the eve of her birthday. "I need you to do me a favor, Hunter."

He grunted.

"I need you to keep Chase out of my room until after midnight."

It was 11:45 p.m., and Chase walked the hospital corridor like a caged tiger.

If he didn't love Lexi so much, he'd charge into her room and tell her how outrageous she was for trying to keep him out. Using his own brother, no less. Chase was going to exchange serious words with him when this was all over.

In some twisted way, Chase was thankful the woman he loved had someone else on her side to protect her. Just not to protect her from *him*.

Hunter stood sentry outside of Lexi's door. Arms crossed, stone-faced and completely impervious to any threat Chase made.

But that was okay.

Hunter wasn't the leader of this platoon. He just didn't know it yet.

As frustrated as Chase was when Hunter put his foot down and wouldn't let him visit Lexi, her ridiculous request lined up nicely with his battle plan. He could wait. He would wait.

Until now.

The Stimpsons stood in front of him, Mr. Stimpson rubbing the back of his neck. "Son, I'm not sure we should do this."

"Oh, hush." Mrs. Stimpson swatted her husband on the arm. "We are totally doing this. All that's required of you is to stand out of sight."

A smile cracked across Mr. Stimpson's face, and he held his hand out to shake Chase's. "I was always a sucker for a good love story. We're rooting for you."

Chase glanced at the clock on the wall. "It's go-time, Mrs. Stimpson. You're up."

The elderly woman pinched her cheeks several times. "This gives some color to my face for dramatic effect." And with that, she scurried down the hall to Hunter.

Chase desperately wanted to watch Mrs. Stimpson wrap Hunter around her finger. Instead, he hightailed it around the square that made up the ward where Lexi's room was located.

Once Chase arrived at the opposite side of the floor, he edged toward the hallway entrance and heard Mrs. Stimpson. "Hunter, they were admitting him to the ER when I left. I don't know what happened. One minute Chase was helping me get coffee and the next he fell to the ground."

Chase heard Hunter's concerned grunt.

"Mr. Stimpson stayed with him and said to come get you." Mrs. Stimpson added in an out-of-breath voice, "So much blood."

Chase bit his fist, trying to get rid of the laughter that wanted to bubble out of his chest. She was giving an Academy Award–winning performance.

Hunter mumbled something to the woman, and they headed to the elevator.

When the elevator doors closed, Chase glanced at the clock in the hallway. Thirteen minutes until her birthday. He slipped into Lexi's room.

Once inside, he leaned a shoulder against the wall, crossed

his arms and stared at the patient. The most beautiful patient he'd ever seen.

Lexi had the decency to look guilty.

"I didn't realize you were so close to my brother," Chase said.

"Apparently, not close enough."

"What'd you offer him in return?"

She slid her eyes to the side. "I was going to set up his small business account for the therapy dogs with a tax program to help him with his quarterly reports."

He raised an eyebrow. "Using Gardner Economics against me?"

"Something like that." Her attention fell to the digital clock on her wall. She knew time was running out just as well as he did.

He hated seeing her in a hospital gown. Absolutely hated it. But anything was better than her pale face and curled-up body he'd held in his arms two days ago.

But here, the smell of tension smothered the medicinal hospital scent. Chase felt like he could choke on it. He needed to guide them to a different place, but he wanted the stress behind her eyes to ease first.

"Your mother's not always a pleasant woman," he said of Clara Gardner.

With one glance at the clock, Lexi said, "My mom's not entirely pleased with me."

"Hunter offered to teach her to repair the fence at the back of the property."

A smile came with a quiet giggle from Lexi.

Good. He had her laughing.

"She'd be a piece of work on that land," she said.

"Doesn't matter." He grinned. "She'd be preoccupied."

While the pressure had ruptured in the room, it still felt heavy. He lowered his voice. "How are you, honey?"

She swallowed and winced slightly, a reminder to Chase of the tube she'd had down her throat just two days ago during a longer-than-expected surgery to clean up the rampant infection from her burst appendix. "I'm okay," she said.

He splayed his hands on his hips, hanging them off his pressed jeans. Well. Pressed jeans twelve hours ago. After sitting in the waiting room and, alternately, pacing several thousand steps, they looked closer to his everyday pairs. Not exactly how he wanted to look on his wedding day.

And yet, somehow Lexi in her hospital gown was perfect. Her face still glowed with beauty, and her eyes told a story he didn't ever want to end.

But they needed to cover a few topics first.

"You want to tell me why you were so sick that we almost lost you, but you didn't share with anyone that you weren't feeling well?"

"I didn't—"

Unable to be far from her for any longer, he took three strides, sat on her bed and gently took her into his arms. He worried he was crushing her, but couldn't help himself. "You scared me to death," he whispered into her hair.

When he released her, she drew back and said, "I was just so out of sorts. I thought my birthday was making me sick. I didn't think anything was wrong."

"You scared me to death," he repeated.

"I know." She put her hand on his forearm. "I know. And I'm so sorry. That's what I want to say to you. I'm so sorry. You had to bring me to the hospital, and that was probably so hard on you."

"Let me get this straight." He bent lower so he could look her in the eyes and understand if he heard correctly. "*Your* appendix burst and *you're* apologizing to *me*? It seems like you've got this wrong."

"Maybe." She looked over his shoulder then back at him. "But the thing you got wrong, Chase, is that you actually considered my marriage proposal."

"What? What are you talking about?" This time he was the one who glanced at the clock. This conversation just took a turn he wasn't sure time would allow.

She shook her head. "Can you sit back a few feet? I think this would be easier if I could explain it to you without being in such close proximity."

He narrowed his eyes at her. "I'm fine where I am." He wasn't going to give her space. If he had anything to do with it, he wouldn't give her space for the next fifty years.

But the feeling coming off Lexi said she had other ideas. He stayed where he was and braced for her words.

She picked at a stray thread on her blanket, and her voice became small. "I'm releasing you from my proposal."

Something metal clamped onto his heart. He steeled his voice. "Why?"

"Because I can't ask you to do that for me."

"Why not?"

She swallowed and looked straight into his eyes, her brown ones pooling with tears. "Because," she whispered, "I accidentally fell in love with you."

The grip on his heart released, and he took a beat to let her words soak into his bones. She fell in love with him. He kept his voice calm. "Good."

"Good?"

"Yes. Good." He took a breath, the space over his heart filling with something foreign. Something warm. Something peaceful. For the first time in four weeks, he could fill his lungs to capacity. "Perfect, in fact."

Her beautiful eyes blinked repeatedly, confusion crossing her brow. "Good that I'm releasing you from my proposal?"

"Yes." He nodded. He hated how torn she looked, but all would become clear in just a few moments. He stood and pulled a small velvet box out of his pocket.

This morning, he wasn't sure if it was wise to take extra time to shop for and purchase a ring, but he took the risk. When he showed up and Vance was in her room, he thought he'd chosen wrong and that the extra time away from the hospital might have cost him Lexi. But hearing of her love for him and seeing her stare at the box, he knew he'd chosen correctly.

He knelt on one knee, ignoring the hard floor, and said, "Don't be angry with me, Lexi."

"Angry?" she squeaked.

His lips lifted in a small grin. "I didn't have time to find a coupon for this purchase. I hope that doesn't make you too angry to answer my question."

Her mouth gaped, but nothing came out.

When he opened the box, a beautiful platinum band displayed a square-cut diamond. A stunning, no-frills diamond, for a stunning, no-frills woman.

"Now that you've recanted your proposal," he said, putting his heart on the line, "maybe you can accept mine. Alexis Jane Gardner, will you marry me?"

She touched her fingertips to her lips. "Marry you?"

"Will you argue with me for the rest of our lives?"

She blinked.

"Will you teach our kids Gardner Economics?"

"You want kids?" she breathed, her question lined with hope.

He nodded.

"I didn't think I'd ever get to have kids," she said on a sob.

"Will you wear matching shirts with me like the Stimpsons when we grow old?"

"The Stimpsons?"

A tear drew down her cheek, and he gently thumbed it away. "They're out in the lobby right now in blue-and-white-checked button-downs."

A single laugh bubbled out of her. But then her face fell. She wrapped her hands around his and the box he was still holding. "I can't marry you, Chase."

He studied her face. She loved him. He knew it. So that wasn't the problem. "Did you already marry Vance?" he asked. "Because if so, he does not look like a happy groom."

Her face broke in shock, and she barked out a laugh this time. "No. I did not marry Vance."

The heaviness of getting married had weighed on her far too long. And while he was again glad to lighten the mood, he still had to get to the root of the problem. He gentled his voice. "Then why can't you marry me, honey?"

"Chase, you don't want to get married again. As much as I love you, I can't ask you to be something you aren't."

He stood, edged his hip onto the side of the mattress and sat beside her on the bed. After placing the ring on her bedside table, he took her face in his hands and pressed his forehead against hers. "And what if I do love you? Am I allowed to change my mind and say I want to get married again? To you?"

Slowly, so slowly it was almost painful for Chase to wait, she pulled back and looked at him. Her eyes perused his face, searching. He waited, trying to remind himself to breathe.

"Why are you saying this now?" she asked.

"Someday," he said quietly, "I'll tell you a story about how God moved a mountain."

"But what changed?"

"I can't live my life looking for guarantees. At some point, I have to trust."

She looked down at her hands, then back to him. The most gorgeous smile broke across her face. "Yes. I will marry you."

He nodded, knowing the battle wasn't over, but so very happy that they'd gotten this far. One glance told him he only had a few minutes remaining to make his point.

Before he put the ring on her finger, or kissed this beautiful woman, he said, "And there's one more thing."

Her eyes darted around the room, as if something or someone was going to jump out at her. And, in a sense, his next request might feel like it.

"I want you to marry me tonight. At 12:01 a.m."

"Chase, what are you talking about? You know—" she shook her head "—you know that tomorrow is my birthday. We have to get married before midnight to save the ranch. There's a pastor in the waiting room. Let's do it now. We say 'I do,' sign the papers and it's done. It would take two minutes, and everything is solved."

That thing in his heart squeezed. She was ridiculously generous. But her generosity might kill their marriage before it started.

"I won't marry you a minute before 12:01." He pulled the marriage license out of his back pocket, unfolded the paper and placed it on her hospital tray. He pounded a pen flush to the top of it and left his palm covering both pen and paper. "We aren't signing this until it's officially tomorrow."

She leaned back, her head turning from marriage license

to him. Once more to the papers and then back to him. "I don't understand."

"Lexi, if we get married before midnight, you'll always wonder if I did it for the money."

"No. I won't. I'll…" When her voice trailed off, she looked at him, her face full of hurt. "Is that what you think of me?"

"No," he said in a tone that brooked no argument. "Not in any way. But we can't risk this. We can't risk that at some point in time, this money becomes a third wheel in our marriage. We have to know, both of us, without a doubt, that we got married because we love each other."

She looked toward the clock. To the paper. Back to him.

He left his palm on the marriage license and pen. "You once told me that you needed the price of gas to go down and a universal charger that crossed electronic brands."

She released something between a laugh and a sob. "How can you remember all of that?"

"I think I remember everything you've said to me since the moment we met," he whispered.

She leaned in and placed her hand on his cheek, pulling him to her and resting her forehead against his.

"I can't give any of that to you, honey. And I can't marry you for your money." He brushed a lock of hair from her cheek to behind her ear. "But I can give you something more important."

"What's that?"

"I can give you the knowledge that you were chosen—" he brushed his lips against hers "—just for who you are."

"Because you treasure me." Her voice trembled.

"Yes," he said. Relief filled his chest. She got it. She finally understood.

"But what about the ranch? We have an opportunity to do good things with that money."

"Lexi." He pulled back. "Do you trust me? Do you trust God? Because that's the choice we get. I can't solve everything financial right now. But I refuse to marry you if it has anything to do with that money."

Her head moved in small, quick shakes, and he shifted his hands away from her face. "But my second cousin."

"That's not up to us. The only thing that's up to us right now is this. Will you marry me? At 12:01 a.m.? And not a minute sooner?"

"This is absurd," she whispered.

"I know, honey. I know that Gardner Economics does not understand this. But marrying me cannot be about an equation. It has to be about our love for each other."

He took her hand and pressed it over his on the license and pen, then he covered their hands with his free one. They turned to watch the clock, their heads pressed together.

11:59.

His breathing sped up to match hers. Their hearts somehow knew they were running down the aisle to each other. And it would only be a few seconds longer.

"I love you, Chase."

The clock struck midnight.

"Happy Birthday, Alexis." He pulled back and took her face in his hands. He touched his lips to hers, promising her everything he had to give her.

"Ahem."

Lexi ran her hands through Chase's hair while he continued to kiss her.

"I don't think they care we're in here," someone murmured.

"I don't think they even know we're in here," another voice said.

Someone coughed. "Most grooms kiss their brides after

the wedding. Do you want me to perform this ceremony now, or should I come back?"

Chase couldn't help his smile. He brushed a final kiss to Lexi's forehead and pulled back. She peeked around him. "We're really getting married now?"

"Only if you want to," he said, feeling so much love for the woman in front of him, he hardly knew what to do with it all. "I have a crew of people ready to put on a midnight wedding in the chapel."

She grinned up at him, making him want to kiss her all over again. "Yes, please," she said.

Within thirty seconds, the room flooded with friends and family. Chase carefully resituated himself next to his fiancée on her hospital bed and watched the scurry of people.

"Where did everyone come from?" Lexi asked.

He wrapped an arm around her. "I might have made some calls."

"They showed for me at midnight?" she asked in disbelief.

He squeezed her shoulder. "This town doesn't look at you as just an integral part of Gardner Economics. You're one of their own."

She put her hand over his and studied each person in the room, a look of awe and wonder on her face.

Alison Velasquez entered with a two-tiered white cake. "White chocolate on the inside with vanilla frosting on the outside." She placed the cake on a small table in the corner of the room. "And we can't forget this." After digging into the pocket of her jacket, she pulled out a plastic bride and groom and gently pushed them into the top of the thick frosting.

"That bride needs a different kind of gown. A hospital gown," Lexi said on a smile.

"But you do have a veil," Alison said as she scooted around people to get to Lexi. "I sew on the side and had an extra that hasn't been purchased yet."

"Let me help with that." Lexi's mother took the shoulder-length, three-layer veil. She had a brush at the ready and worked through Lexi's hair, then attached the veil comb to the top of her daughter's head. When she pulled back to inspect her work, a sheen of tears lined her eyes. "Is it okay that I'm here?" she whispered.

Lexi took her mother's hand in hers. "I wouldn't want to get married without you present."

The florist flitted around the room, attaching red rose boutonnieres to the men and handing long-stemmed singles to the women. She pulled out a huge bouquet of cream-colored calla lilies, bound by a silky cream ribbon. "Fresh and new," she whispered when she handed them to Lexi.

Someone caught Lexi's eye, and Chase followed her line of sight.

Frank wedged himself into the corner of the room, a 35mm camera hung around his neck by a woven strap that belonged back in the seventies.

"What is your foreman doing?" she asked Chase quietly, though not quietly enough.

Frank looked at Lexi. "I know more than just cows and fertilizer."

She giggled.

"He's the photographer for the wedding. He took most of the pictures in the lodge." Including the shot of Laura skiing downhill. Chase filled with warmth. There was something beautiful about Frank being here for this moment, too.

"I brought you a present," Hunter announced from the door.

"I'm not sure I want anything from you," Chase said

in all seriousness, though everyone in the room chuckled. This group had had a front row seat to Hunter standing guard at Lexi's door.

"You'll want this," his twin said.

Their sister, Cora, peeked her head into the room.

Chase stood with his mouth open. It had been too long since he'd seen her. Her hair had grown and now covered the scar he knew was there, and her eyes told of a maturity he'd never seen in his little sister.

He got off the bed and engulfed her in a hug. "I'm so glad you're here," he whispered into her hair, his voice thick.

"I wouldn't miss this for the world." She pulled back, but kept a grip on his arms. "I wish Mom and Dad could be here."

"Yeah," he said. The space in his heart where only his parents lived squeezed.

"But I have something that puts them in the room with us." She shoved her hand into her jeans pocket and pulled out their father's wedding band. She set the ring in his palm.

He could only stare at it. "I don't know what to say."

"There's nothing needed to say," she replied softly. Then she took her voice up a notch and said to the room, "Are we going to have a wedding or what? I told Gretel Heard I couldn't deliver her daughter's baby until my brother got married, and she wasn't too happy. Let's get this show on the road."

Everyone chuckled, but Chase knew better. She'd drop him faster than a hot pan off the stove if a patient needed her.

He glanced around the crowd, but didn't find the other face he was looking for.

Hunter clapped him on the shoulder. His twin said quietly, "Couldn't get a hold of him."

Chase nodded once. He wouldn't let Ryder's absence ruin his wedding day.

"Age before beauty," Mrs. Stimpson said as she pushed through everyone to get to the end of Lexi's hospital bed.

Hunter scowled at the elderly woman and her husband. "You two have a lot to answer for."

Mrs. Stimpson stuck her nose in the air. "I'll do no such thing. If the roles were reversed, Hunter Cross, I would have done the same for you."

"I take it there's a story behind that comment?" Lexi asked Chase.

"I'll tell you later." Chase took his place next to his bride. "Suffice it to say, the Stimpsons played a role in getting me into your room."

Lexi smiled at Mrs. Stimpson. "I can't believe you're both here so late."

"Are you kidding? This is the most excitement I've had since Louella hot-wired Henry Gunner's scooter and took a joy ride through Bright Horizons."

Lexi's mother's mouth gaped. She clutched at her necklace. "My mother-in-law stole someone's scooter?"

Mrs. Stimpson grinned. "Stick around, and I'll tell you more stories you won't believe."

Nurse Julie tromped into Lexi's room.

"I thought you were off tonight," Lexi said.

"I *am* off," she said, crossing her arms. "Because if I was *on*, I would have to care about visitor hours and visitor capacity. But as of right now, I'm attending the wedding of a new friend. A new friend who needs her rest and therefore needs this to be the shortest wedding in the history of wedding ceremonies."

Pastor Gentry nodded to Julie and cleared his throat.

"All right. Could everyone please proceed to the chapel and take your places?"

And with Chase standing to the right of the stage, in the dim light of the small hospital chapel, he watched as Lexi's mother pushed Lexi's wheelchair. Her mother on one side and the IV stand on the other, with a smile so big he wondered if it hurt her, Lexi slowly made her way down the short aisle to him. She was radiant. And he couldn't believe he was going to get to marry this woman.

After exchanging *I do*s, rings and short vows, they toasted apple juice, ate cake and finally signed the wedding license.

At 12:37 a.m.

Chapter Thirteen

Sun streamed through the blinds of Lexi's hospital room, begging her to see what the new day would bring.

Her birthday. Her thirty-fifth birthday.

In all her years of knowing what this particular birthday meant, she never imagined she would wake up to the sight in front of her.

She couldn't take her eyes off her sleeping husband. Hair tousled. Stubble shadowing his strong jaw. Legs stretched out long and boots crossed at the ankles. Arms also crossed, but against his chest, somehow making his shoulders appear wider, able to carry whatever burden came their way.

With slow blinks, a yawn and a stretch of his arms over his head, Chase awoke. He focused his eyes on her. "How are you feeling this morning, honey?"

"Wonderful," she said softly.

He pushed out of his chair and sat next to her on the bed. He took her hands in his and brushed his lips against hers. Sweet. Gentle. "Good morning, beautiful." His voice was thick with sleep and affection.

Heat hit her face, and it took her a second to understand what she was feeling. Something bashful seemed to flitter across her nerves.

"Don't blush," he whispered in her ear as he slipped his

arms around her. "I'm your husband now. I get to tell you how pretty you are as often as I want."

She laughed, part nervous, part practical. "I'm in a hospital gown with my arm hooked up to an IV. Not to sound critical, but I think your bar is a little low."

He pulled back and grinned. "We've got to bust you out of this joint. And soon."

"Amen to that."

Her ringtone sounded from the bedside table.

Chase pulled her phone off her charger and handed it to her. When she saw who was calling on the display, she blanched. "It's my lawyer."

"Better take that, honey." He nodded to her and held her eyes in his. "It'll be okay. You can tell him what happened, and we'll figure the rest out. In the meantime, I have a small wedding gift for you. But you can't peek while I'm getting it set up."

She furrowed her brows at her husband, but hit the screen to answer, turned the call to speaker, then laid the phone between them. "Hi, Mr. Morton."

Chase positioned himself at the foot of the bed and proceeded to pull the covers up over her feet, bunching them so high she couldn't see what he was doing.

"Lexi, I'm sorry to call so early." Mr. Morton's voice sounded through the phone speaker. "But the lawyer representing the trust contacted me first thing and wanted an update on your situation."

A squeeze of her foot from her husband fortified her. "Well, I have some good news, Mr. Morton, but it might not be what you think." She smiled, and looking straight into Chase's hazel eyes, she said, "I got married last night."

Chase grinned back at her and removed her socks.

Mr. Morton started to congratulate her, but she interrupted him, still smiling and staring into her husband's beautiful eyes. "We didn't get married before midnight, Mr. Morton."

While silence came from the other end of the line, Chase turned, blocking her view from what he was doing. Mr. Morton finally said, "I don't understand."

"We got married after midnight. The trust fund will have to go to someone else."

More silence. With the hospital covers still blocking her view, Chase slipped a pair of socks onto her feet. Lexi sat up straight.

She hit Mute on the phone. "I want to see," she said to Chase urgently.

"Patience." He held on to the railing and made movements that looked like he was toeing off his boots. When Lexi tried to peek around the bed to see what he was doing, he held up his hand to signal her to stop.

She rolled her eyes playfully and unmuted the phone. "Mr. Morton, are you still there?"

"Hang on, Ms. Gardner."

"It's Mrs. Cross now, Mr. Morton." Chase's gaze heated, and she winked.

"Hang on, Mrs. Cross." Lexi could hear what sounded like papers shuffling in the background of the call but was distracted when Chase sat next to her on the bed.

"Scooch over," he muttered quietly.

When she made room for him, in one fell swoop, he slung his legs parallel to hers on the bed and yanked the covers off her feet.

Thick white socks covered her feet, pink letters across her toes spelling the word "Wife." On Chase's feet were the matching set with dark blue letters that spelled the word "Husband."

She burst out laughing and wrapped her arms around his neck. "I can't believe you did this."

"Ms. Gard—Mrs. Cross?" her lawyer called from the phone.

Tamping down her giggles, Lexi answered, "Sorry, Mr. Morton. We're here."

"What time was it you got married?"

"It doesn't matter. It was after midnight."

"I understand. But what time was it? Exactly?"

Chase snagged the marriage license off the tray table and held it in front of them.

This conversation was trying its best to dampen her first day as a married woman. But she wouldn't let it. Her lawyer must have to document all the details to pass the information on and close his file. She could respect that. "Our marriage license says we were officially married at 12:37 a.m."

"What time zone?"

"Mountain," she replied.

More silence. Lexi shrugged at Chase. She had no idea why this was taking so long. Chase took her hand in his. He thumbed the new rings on her finger. During the ceremony, he'd added a thin band circled with tiny diamonds.

"Mrs. Cross, the trust clearly states you had to be married by 11:59 p.m.—"

"Yes, I know."

"—Pacific time."

This time the silence was on her end. Slowly, both Chase and Lexi lifted their gaze from their joined hands to each other.

"What did you just say?" she asked, not taking her eyes from Chase, his face filled with the same expression of confusion and disbelief that no doubt filled her own.

"You had to be married by 11:59 p.m. on the eve of your thirty-fifth birthday, Pacific time."

"Lexi…" Her name trailed off Chase's tongue.

She could feel herself blinking rapidly. She knew she should say something. But her brain couldn't register his words.

"You were married at 12:37 a.m. Mountain time, which was 11:37 p.m. Pacific time. You successfully fulfilled the stipulations of the trust."

Mr. Morton continued to ramble instructions to Lexi. Something about filing the license with the state and getting it to him as soon as possible. Something else about proper channels and granting her access to the account.

Lexi couldn't be entirely sure about any of those details because she was preoccupied with kissing Chase Cross. Her husband.

Epilogue

"**D**uke!" Chase whistled across the field, hoping his dog would respond to him. In the last year, Duke had all but abandoned his loyalties to Chase and vowed his life to Lexi. But the way Duke had been circling his wife the last few weeks gave him pause.

What was wrong with his dog?

For that matter, what was wrong with his wife?

Punctual used to be her middle name. But now he was out looking for her because their impending family dinner would start soon, and she was nowhere to be found. Lately, she'd lost track of time. And seemed a little tired. He'd have to talk to her about her work schedule. Getting the nonprofit up and running while still working with a few accounting clients had taken its toll.

Lexi exited a trail coming from a cabin. No doubt she was welcoming the latest army veteran and his wife. They came to Four Cross Ranch with both their car and relationship on fumes. He prayed the ranch could offer them refuge and hope.

Chase's wife caught sight of him and waved.

She walked toward him, his dog pasted to her side. When she got to him, she lifted on tiptoes and kissed him. She smelled of wildflowers, his land and a life full of love.

Duke bumped Chase's hand, almost as if to push him away.

"What is wrong with you, Duke?"

Lexi giggled. "Nothing's wrong with him. He's just protective."

"From me?" He looked at Duke and said, "That makes no sense."

"It might soon," Lexi muttered, looking at her dog, a smile on her lips.

"You've been a little tired lately, so I thought I'd bring you a pick-me-up before family dinner." He handed her the travel mug of coffee he had in tow. "With peppermint. Just how you like it."

She looked at the mug, her brow a touch furrowed. "Oh, thanks. I'll just wait for it to cool down some."

"How are the Hensons?" he asked of the latest veteran family as he took her hand in his to walk toward the parking lot.

"Settled in." She glanced back to Chase. "What's going on with Hunter? I saw him working on the back side of the property earlier today. Did you banish him to fence repair?"

"He's pouting." She raised her eyebrows, and he explained. "Sheila told him she's engaged to her high school boyfriend. Happened right under his nose. He's so miserable to be around, he sent himself out to work the fence."

"I hate that he's upset. I think he enjoyed her company, but he was never quite committed to her."

"I don't think he knows what he wants." Chase shook his head. His brother had been tight-lipped. "I told him he had to be on his best behavior tonight, though."

Walking their way off property to the parking lot, they closed the gate and left Duke on the opposite side to stay at the ranch while they dined. He paced back and forth, yelping at them every time he turned. Chase shook his head. Seriously. What was going on with his dog?

When they reached the parking lot, Lexi shaded her eyes with her hand and looked around. "Where's my car?"

"Over here." Chase led her to the side of the lot and stood them in front of a silver Ford F-150 Lightning truck.

She stared at him. "I don't understand."

Grinning, he pulled the key fob out of his pocket, held it out for her to see and beeped the locks open.

Her eyes grew wide. "What did you do?"

"Don't be mad," he said, unable to contain his smile.

She put a hand over her mouth and shook her head. "What did you do?"

"I am a very patient man. I waited a long time for you to purchase a vehicle suitable for Wyoming winters and terrain." She opened her mouth to respond, but he held his hand up. "Before you say anything, do I need to mention how many times we've pulled you out of a ditch?"

She shook her head once. His wife was cute.

"A buddy of mine inherited this truck, among other things, when his dad died. He and his brothers all clocked military time. Some fared better than others. He sold the truck to me discounted in exchange for weeks at the ranch for his and his brothers' families. But I might have accidentally written him a check for the full amount anyway."

She threw her arms around him. "You are officially a master at Gardner Economics."

"I learned from the best." He opened the driver's-side door, and Lexi climbed into the seat. "I need my girl in a safe ride."

"For more reasons than you know." She beamed a smile at him.

He thought he had learned all of Lexi's smiles. Light of

the morning smile. Glad to see him smile. Her mischievous smiles that always threw him off. But this one—he didn't recognize this smile. And yet his nerve endings buzzed at the sight of it.

Lexi shifted her weight so she could pull something out of her back pocket. "If we're doing random gifts now, you should open this." She handed him a small card. "I made it myself." She licked her lips. "I mean, I had help. But it's homemade."

Whatever was in this card made his wife's cheeks pink. He ripped the envelope open and saw the contents. His entire body froze.

"I also got you these." Her voice quivered, and she placed a pair of socks in his hand. Across the toes in black letters read the word "Daddy."

With a picture of a sonogram in one hand and a pair of socks declaring his fatherhood in the other, he looked at his wife. His beautiful, beaming, pregnant-woman-who-his-dog-is-protecting wife.

Chase stepped flush to the truck, slid his hands around Lexi and buried his face in her hair.

"Thank you for the truck, Chase. Now your girls," she whispered, "or your girl and your boy, will have a safe ride."

He didn't want to squeeze her too hard, but they stayed embraced for as long as he could manage before they headed to the restaurant. The entire night Chase spent glued to his wife. He felt unsettled if he wasn't connected to her in some way. An arm around her chair, a hand playing with her hair, their fingers intertwined.

He and his dog were about to come to blows to see who got to be by Lexi's side for the next nine months.

Chase paid the bill, and they walked Hunter and Cora to the front of the restaurant.

"Happy for you, man." Hunter clapped Chase on the shoulder, then lowered his voice. "I don't think I ever want my own, but you're happy. Lexi's happy. All of that is good."

Before Chase could address his brother's surprising comment, Hunter grinned and said, "Aren't you glad we didn't hire the old man accountant?"

Lexi sent Chase a questioning look. He squeezed her to his side. "I never considered hiring anyone other than you."

Cora approached and went up on tiptoe to kiss him on the cheek.

"Thanks for coming to dinner, Cora." Lexi leaned into his sister for a hug.

"I'm thrilled for you." She pulled back but didn't let go of Lexi's arms. "I'm going to be an aunt," she squealed.

Lexi laughed and rubbed her flat stomach. "I'm hoping you'll be one of the first to meet this little one. Would you feel comfortable helping with the delivery?"

"I'm always up for a delivery." Chase knew that was the truth. "But you'll have to come off that ranch for me to deliver your baby." Cora flicked her hand out in farewell, and Hunter walked her to her car.

A tired Lexi insisted Chase drive the new truck home. Within three minutes, she'd fallen asleep.

With his sleeping wife, carrying his baby, they drove past his mountain and straight home. To Four Cross Ranch.

* * * * *

Dear Reader,

Welcome to Four Cross Ranch! Thank you for letting me share Chase and Lexi's journey with you. I've always been intrigued with marriage of convenience stories. What would it really take for two people to honor each other and fall in love under those circumstances? Apparently, it takes a grumpy hero, a generous heroine and a dog who knows where his loyalty lies.

Like Chase, we all have our mountains standing in front of us. Life's wounds stare us in the face and can paralyze our hearts and minds. That was certainly the case for both Chase and Lexi. Moving forward and grasping what God has for us on the other side of pain can be scary. But we have a trustworthy God who will move that mountain for us. And for that I am forever grateful.

I hope you enjoyed your visit to Four Cross Ranch. Head on over to my website at deborahclack.com and sign up for my newsletter to get updates on Hunter's, Cora's and Ryder's stories. I also have a free novella for you to tide you over until our next visit to Wyoming.

One last note: For years I wrote books, praying for and wondering who my readers would be someday. With this as my first published work, it's you! You're the reader! And it's so fun that it's you. Know that you are loved and prayed for.

Sincerely,
Deborah